# C.R.E.A.M 3

Yolanda Moore

**Lock Down Publications and Ca$h Presents**
# C.R.E.A.M. 3
**A Novel by *Yolanda Moore***

Yolanda Moore

**Lock Down Publications**
P.O. Box 944
Stockbridge, Ga 30281

**Visit our website @**
www.lockdownpublications.com

Copyright 2022 by Yolanda Moore
C.R.E.A.M. 3

All rights reserved. No part of this book may be reproduced in any form or by electronic or mechanical means, including information storage and retrieval systems without permission in writing from the publisher, except by a reviewer who may quote brief passages in review.
First Edition July 2022
Printed in the United States of America

*This is a work of fiction. Names, characters, places, and incidents either are products of the author's imagination or are used fictitiously. Any similarity to actual events or locales or persons, living or dead, is entirely coincidental.*

**Lock Down Publications**
**Like our page on Facebook: Lock Down Publications @**
www.facebook.com/lockdownpublications.ldp

Cover design and layout by: **Dynasty Cover Me**
Book interior design by: **Shawn Walker**
Edited by: **Cassandra Barrett-Sims**

C.R.E.A.M. 3

## Stay Connected with Us!

Text **LOCKDOWN** to 22828 to stay up-to-date with new releases, sneak peaks, contests and more…
Thank you.

Yolanda Moore

## **Submission Guideline.**

Submit the first three chapters of your completed manuscript to ldpsubmissions@gmail.com, subject line: Your book's title. The manuscript must be in a .doc file and sent as an attachment. Document should be in Times New Roman, double spaced and in size 12 font. Also, provide your synopsis and full contact information. If sending multiple submissions, they must each be in a separate email.

Have a story but no way to send it electronically? You can still submit to LDP/Ca$h Presents. Send in the first three chapters, written or typed, of your completed manuscript to:

LDP: Submissions Dept
P.O. Box 944
Stockbridge, Ga 30281

*DO NOT send original manuscript. Must be a duplicate.*

Provide your synopsis and a cover letter containing your full contact information.

Thanks for considering LDP and Ca$h Presents.

# C.R.E.A.M. 3

## ACKNOWLEDGEMENTS

I would first like to thank my Heavenly Father for being so good to me, words can't even describe. To my grandmother: Cora J. Warner: Thank you for being my strength and for keeping the telephone to heaven ringing so I can always place a prayer request for myself. Thank you for being the person I could call morning, noon, or night during my incarceration journey.

To my children: Miracle Jaishawn and Nasir Malik: My wish for you is that you never give up on yourselves because I never will. No matter what, remember, I love you, even when momma fussing at you. I am proud of the both of you and I'm glad to call you *my children*. I love you more, I loved you first, and I love you still.

To all my cousins, aunts, uncles, nieces, and nephews: I love you. Latoya, Larry, Kiva, Trina, Markal, and all my sisters and one brother, I love y'all too.

To my friends Ashley London and Adrienne Johnson: What would I do without you bitches? I don't know, and I surely don't want to find out.

Niketra Deloach: You are a pain in my spine. No, really you are, which is why we've spent the last two days, so far, without saying one word to each other (smile). I wouldn't trade yo' ugly ass for nothing in the world though. I love you, and thanks for helping me push this book through.

To my Fans: Who am I without you? Certainly not an author, so thanks for all the love and support. It is because of you I am becoming someone great. Thanks.

Yolanda Moore

# PROLOGUE

I dabbed the sweat beading above my top lip with the back of my hand. I really wished I was doing something else right now. Instead, I was at my desk contemplating if I should write this for my children. The more I thought about leaving my children to have to fend for themselves in this cold world, the more my stomach sank. I picked up my pink pen, the pink sparkly one A'Miracle loved to play with and willed myself to write the words embedded in my heart. I was really struggling to get them down on paper. I felt as though writing down my thoughts would be saying fuck life rather than continuing to be the soulja Ann created.

*I'm a fighter. So, what am I doing here?* It was as if I was ready to give in. My kids deserved more right now. This, what I was doing, wasn't a consideration of suicide. I wouldn't dare commit the ultimate sin against myself and God, but if I couldn't get up and fight, then I might as well have been the fuckin' flop everyone was claiming me to be.

"Quit being a pussy," I said aloud, trying to gain control of the emotion as it oozed out of my pores like an infectious disease.

"Just write the book, Cache. Only two things can happen in the trenches ... kill or be killed," I said, having a full-fledged conversation with myself. I began to write despite what my heart told me. If I had to leave this world I wanted my children to have the realest, most honest truth. The one thing I had found out was that money didn't always bring you happiness. Maybe in the moment, but once it was all said and done, money couldn't buy me love or happiness. The streets had taken away what I loved.

*Identity* was the first word I wrote down to begin my story. My memoir. Just in case. So, I started to jot my thoughts down. It began: *Dead, gone rapt, absent, astray. Damned, doomed, vanished, desperate and destroyed. Everything I feel: VOID.* I always knew this would be life for me, especially with all I had taken in as a child. Still, I fought for the better ... my better. I fought so hard with unannounced strength, but still, I headed into destruction. With no guidance (someone who leads or directs another) to tell me the fight I fought was against myself. I was faced with another me, someone I would like to label a beast, but didn't know how to defeat myself.

Because the scripture: "the truth shall set you free," was something I had been taught early in life, it was embedded in me, yet I was too ashamed to admit the things I had done in the dark. I robbed, I stole, and I committed adultery. I was so ashamed of myself ... lack of self-confidence with no confidence.

At the age of fourteen is when it all started, and I had taken a left turn long before I was granted the chance of adolescence. I'd had my first experience with consuming drugs, but it seemed I was destined for havoc long before that. You would've thought I knew better. I watched my mom and dad, your grandparents, go through some horrific things in life, suffering through addiction. Seeing them do drugs and drink alcohol, which caused them to lose their lives at a young age, apparently wasn't enough for me.

My drug addiction, in a way, had caused me to lose a lot too. Hope, preservation, truth, and so on. I'm grateful that I'm able to see and overcome what my parents could not—and that is to defeat the stronghold of addiction. What helped me faithfully through my recovery when I was in prison was the Eight Beatitudes (R.E.C.O.V.E.R.Y).

Here is my story on how I gained the whole world just to lose it.

## C.R.E.A.M. 3

*1)*     *Realize I'm not God. I admit that I am powerless to control my tendency to do the wrong things and that my life is unmanageable.* "Happy are those who know they are spiritually poor" (Matt 5:3).

Life started moving for me in a promiscuous way, too recklessly. Looking for what I lacked ... LOVE. Men and drugs became my antidote and even women too, but above all Xanax and coke were my GODs, cleansing and washing away the sins that sustained my skin. My drug abuse is where I found refuge. With it, it was as if a blanket covered my mind and heart. I felt safe. At least that was what I thought at the moment.

It was a feeling I had never sensed, and I had finally fell in love with myself. I felt as if there was an aura about me that boosted my confidence. I was able to do things I never imagined—like look in the mirror and love what I saw. I was five feet seven and walked with a stride Naomi Campbell couldn't even touch. I started wearing makeup, and little by little, exposing my body. It made me feel superior. No one could tell me anything. I was that bitch.

*2)*     *Earnestly believe that God exists, that I matter to him and that he has the power to help me recover.* "Happy are those who mourn for they shall be comforted" (Matt 5:4).

Yeah, that was until the truth was exposed. By the time I longed to get my life together I had become a mother of two and shit started to get too demanding. You would have thought this would be a time when I ran to the altar and hooked up with the Holy Spirit, but now I was faced with the same blessings and curse that fell upon my mother. I had two beautiful children, but my life had started to crumble like a cookie. I wasn't worried about much though because like I said, drugs had become my ally, my accountability partner.

3) Consciously choose to commit all my life and will to Christ's care and control. "Happy are the meek" (Matt 5:5).

I started to feel as though I wasn't worthy of much in life because I had done the unforgivable to myself. In a flash, my mother's life had become my destiny. I remember trying not to fall into the pits of hell, but somehow I ended up falling directly into her footsteps while taking it all in stride. My life had become a constant simulation and I was trapped inside a landscape of fear, which had converted into my reality. Just like Tris, in the Divergent series, I had become accustomed to life, but knew I didn't belong, but I still fought.

I didn't give up. "God makes no mistakes," is what I told myself constantly, and I knew He had given me the strength to fight with the heart of a lion— all I had to do was hear my roar. At that moment I didn't know what I possessed. With all that said, the thought of it all made me decree the assassination against my demonic entity. All that existed in my past cast an attack on my future before I knew what hit me. I knew I needed to get through and remain standing once the smoke had cleared.

4) Openly examine and confess my faults to myself, to God, and someone I trust. "Happy are the pure in heart" (Matt 5:8).

A future I thought I wouldn't be able to make it through, I was faced with armed robbery, and a murder case over my head I did not commit. I spent several years of my life facing a life sentence. Honestly, I thought I would never fear anything, but I was afraid, which was a feeling I hadn't felt in years. Of course, without self-medicating, I also felt exposed. I became overwhelmed with emotion like when God opened the floodgates of Heaven. I was filled with dread. However, my criminal activity was not on my cranium. All the hurt, the pain, and the abuse I faced was now my challenge. Crying for days had been similar to how a duck takes to water. I remember calling home and telling Momo C.W. how ashamed I was. Without Xanax I was now really able to look in the mirror and see the truth, and not the mirror that showed my physical appearance.

When fighting for my life in the 19th Judicial System was all said and done, I had been sentenced to a fifteen-year sentence of hard labor. I knew I had a lot of work to do. I was determined to walk a different walk to talk a different talk, and this time I didn't need drugs to boost my self-esteem. I had been blessed with charm and I knew exactly how to beat the system.

5) Voluntarily submit to every change God wants to make in my life and humbly ask Him to remove my character defects. "Happy are those whose greatest desire is to do what God requires" (Matt 5:6).

One thing my mother had always taught me was how to survive. So, I considered myself a survivor, an overcomer, and I knew how to endure and outlast everything thrown in my path. I knew to survive I had to always keep on keeping on. See, finding a way to get through the storm was something I never had a problem with. One of my favorite sayings was about dancing and rejoicing in the rain. I had flirted with death for far too long. I wanted to see life— my life through a kaleidoscope, up close and personal. The only way I could do so was if I took time out with myself. So I stopped placing all my hurts and hang-ups on the front line, while carrying everyone else's baggage around, and I looked into the two mirrors of my life's kaleidoscope and examined all my faults. I knew what I had to do. Those loose bits of colored glass had been shattered for far too long. Besides, I knew I couldn't help others if I couldn't help myself.

6) *Evaluate all my relationships.* Offer forgiveness to those who have hurt me and make amends for harm I've done to others, except when to do so would harm them or others. *"Happy are the merciful" (Matt 5:7). "Happy are the peacemakers" (Matt 5:9).*

I had started to forgive everyone who had caused me harm, whether it had been mentally, physically, sexually, or even spiritually. Well let's just say the people who were supposed to have been my protectors hadn't played their parts. Including myself because I realized I had done myself the most harm. Naturally, once I forgave myself I started to heal as if I had touched the hem of God's garment. The relationship between my family and I did a three-sixty, which included my mother with whom my hurt had generated, and her mother as well. However, I cannot just stop there. Asking for forgiveness from the two of you is the hardest, but I know it has to be done. I'm not sure what the future holds for me but I feel this is just as appropriate time as any other. Forgive me of my transgressions? At least, I hope the two of you will find it in your hearts.

As I said, this is a generational curse and our family wears it proudly without even knowing it. Maybe one day you can have a life with kids, a yard with a dog, and a white-picket *fence. Or maybe that only happens on TV shows like "Full House" with Joey, or "The Brady Bunch." What I'm trying to get at is I want the best for my babies as long as it comes in the form of peace, joy, happiness, and most importantly, loyalty. Not love, because love, loves no one but self. Always remember that. And if one of you happens to prove me wrong, then so be it.*

*7) Reserve a daily time with God for self-examination. Bible reading and prayer in order to know God and His will for my life and to gain the power to follow His will.*

*Yes, my first step was admitting I was powerless, but my first step was also cracking open my celebrate recovery workbook and continuing to turn the pages. Well, that was until I had been granted early release. I never made it through the whole 8 steps so if I had to figure things out on my own I would, but the saying 'God forgives not me' ...*

Coming out of my thoughts, I stopped writing the memoir and decided my work here was done. The more I wrote the more I felt as if I was writing my end, as if I was planning my own demise.
"Get it together, Cache," I told myself.
As I stood up, I felt a cold chill throughout my body as if death was creeping around the corner. I made up my mind to go and peek in the room to make sure my kids were sound asleep, and that no harm had come their way. Just when the thought crossed my mind, I heard the wooden floors creak and remembered Tony had made a quick run to the store.
"Fuck." I cursed under my breath so low I barely heard myself. *My gun*, I thought, as I tried to tiptoe through the house. I had left it in the kitchen on top of the island. *So fuckin'*

*reckless of me,* I thought, angry at myself for slipping up like this. But this was the type of shit that happened when you were in your heart wearing your feelings on your sleeve. Everything that was supposed to matter faded. I had been trying so hard to keep my head on straight and stay alive for my children, I had become too engrossed with the fatality of fuckin' up. I just hoped the slip of the mind wouldn't cost me my life.

Just as I crossed the threshold to enter the living room, I saw Knasir standing by the TV with the remote in his hand. Out the corner of my eye I saw a shadow and my heart dropped into my ass.

*Boom! Boom! Boom!* I heard the gunshots. I ran into the direction of the front door. I swung it open and that's when I saw Tony and Maya …

# CHAPTER 1
## TONY

*Boom!* Detective Fernandez slammed his hand down on the stainless steel table as if that shit would intimidate me. What he didn't know was the shit enticed me. *I won't entertain it tho*, I thought as I smirked. I'ma let the nigga hide behind that badge. *Serve and protect my ass*. I shook my head at that fool. *Fuck 'im*, I thought.

I need answers and I need them now!" he shouted, too close for my comfort. He demanded I tell him some shit I knew nothing about.

I didn't know what these bitches wanted from me, but whatever it was, I wasn't the nigga to help them. For as long as I had lived I had never been a good Samaritan and didn't plan on converting to being one anytime soon. Who did that shit besides a muthafucka with a death wish or not a lick of common sense? Niggas be setting themselves up. Then, when they stupid ass get caught with their pants down and locked behind bars, they spent most of their time behind them walls wondering how they ended up in their current situation, hoping the white man changed the law to grant them freedom. Didn't niggas know loose lips sank ships? I damn sure wasn't going to give the next nigga the opportunity to do that shit either.

I refused to become one of those niggas who got sent up state hollin' 'bout how they found God and educating the next nigga on how Allah been good to them, but still sitting in Angola with a lifetime to go.

*What am I sitting here thinking about?* I shook those thoughts from my head knowing I wasn't above getting knocked, 'cause from the looks of it, I could very well become one of those same niggas at any minute. Just 'cause them bitches hadn't read me my rights yet didn't mean they wouldn't. Of course, I prayed they wouldn't. Whatever the fuck they thought they had on me, I was the wrong person. However, that shit ain't never stopped them crooked ass bitches from locking niggas up on bogus charges. Look at Nico Delouch; the man spent thirty years or so at Louisiana State Penitentiary (LSP) and then all of a sudden, all the charges against him had been dropped.

"We found a weapon on your homeboy, Corey Lane, the night he was killed, and guess whose fingerprints were all over that muthafucka?" Fernandez continued to talk. I didn't have a muthafuckin' thang for him, straight up.

"When ballistics came back with two sets of prints and two bodies, but only one dumb muthafucka alive to fall flat on his face, whether you pulled the trigger or not, this one is all for you. Does that shit sound like it's making sense to you?" his hunched-back ass had the nerve to ask, as if I was a dumb muthafucka who would tell him anything. But his across-the-border ass needed to rethink the bullshit ass question he was coming at me with.

"I just came back from your neck of the woods with the wife, but I'm pretty sure you already know that without me even telling you the shit. So with that said, you know muthafuckin' well I don't know what the fuck you talkin' 'bout," I said, knowing even *that* little bit of info was too much talking. Anything I said could be held against me, but I had to give them bitches some kind of alibi. I hated the fuckin' cops and every time I was too close for comfort, my fuckin' nerves were shot. I needed a stiff fuckin' drink and a nigga didn't even drink. I didn't show it though since I was good at keeping a poker face.

"Oh, no, no, no, you were actually here at the time." He smiled at me like he knew something I didn't or as if he was about to get a full confession while I was being recorded. "This occurred right before you and our ride-or-die bitch escaped to Mexico on the run from that murder charge. You know the one I'm talking about … at that fancy hotel downtown. I'm pretty sure right before she blew his brains out he was blowing her back out," he said, smirking, getting to me.

"Bitch, don't you ever disrespect my wife like that!" This time I was the one banging my hand on the metal table, and if he kept it up, it would be his face instead of the table. *Fuck the police!* I thought fuming. I looked into his eyes and gave him a look that could kill if there was such a thing. If he came out the side of his neck one more fuckin' time, I was ready to say fuck it and let them bitch-ass niggas cuff me and throw me in a cell. I didn't plan on saying shit else. This was his fuckin' profession, so his ass should know when he was dealing with a cold-blooded killer. My guns bust just like his. The only difference between the two of us was the fact that I would leave his ass struggling to breathe if he ain't have that badge. I knew plenty niggas like him and they was all bark and no bite.

"*Son*," he said, being sarcastic, "ain't that what you guys refer to each other as?" I had to laugh. The shit was funny. As long as I got my point across I wasn't worried about what that fool was talking about. "Are you ready to go up shit's creek for some street beef? Because that's exactly what's about to happen." He looked at me and shook his head while his ugly face held an even uglier smirk. "No one gives two fucks about you, you know that? Not the struggle, not the streets, or who has the biggest chain on. Y'all young black men kill me with your self-righteous bullshit." Again he shook his head. "By the way, how do you think your *wife* will feel when we give her this little info?"

"The gun is. Not. Mine. And I told you several times I don't know shit. That's all I have for you *son*! Now can I go?"

## Yolanda Moore

I was getting a little angry because I could see the shit that was about to unfold. Them bitches were definitely trying to pen a murder charge on me. Where the fuck was all that coming from? "Tell that shit to somebody else because I don't believe shit you say. Do you know how many muthafuckas like you come in here running the same I-didn't-do-it crap? *I wasn't there!*" he said, trying to mimic me. "You're trying to protect yourself and I understand that, but understand this, I've got a job to do, and I'm gonna do my fuckin' job to the best of my ability by any means. In this world we all have a part to play. Just so happens that in this scenario, we're playing cops and robbers. With that said, you either bullshitin' me or apparently you need to think long and hard about all those bodies under your belt. You think I would just drag you down here to fuck with you? I have better shit to do than ruffle your feathers. The state don't pay me enough for that bullshit, and honestly, the benefits suck. I can promise you I don't waste my time. Now this is my question to you: Do you kill *that* many people that you can't keep up?"

I couldn't help it. I had to laugh dead in that clown's face because at that point he was looking like Bozo. Them muthafuckas would say or do anything to make a nigga conjure up a confession. I shook my head at the measures they'd go through. "Maybe you dragged me down here to see if I knew anything just so you could get a bonus or a pat on the back by the mayor. I can see it now— a plaque and a handshake for a job well done. Not today, big homie."

"Fernandez," cop two called out, patting Fernandez' shoulder. "Give him a little space to breathe. Let me talk to him."

I looked at that clown ass nigga like the comedian he was. What a fuckin' joke. Did he really think it would make a difference who the fuck stayed or went? I had nothing to say to either of them muthafuckas. I knew exactly what the fuck the nigga was trying to pull. Did he think just because he was black we could relate to one another?

I had nothing to say except ... "I want my fuckin' lawyer! Now!"

"Fuck!" He cursed madder than two whores on a Saturday night who couldn't pull a trick if they were fuckin' for free. I sat there smirking.

I knew they wouldn't like it one bit once I made the call and lawyered up on their asses. But like I said, these bitches tried playing on a muthafucka top and I didn't have a gang of defense attorney's for nothing. It was definitely time for them to put in that work and earn their pay from me.

"Damn," I said aloud as soon as they walked out of the room. I thought about Cache. I needed to see her face like yesterday. I knew she was a big girl and this shit wasn't new to her so I knew she knew how to conduct herself in a situation like this. That still didn't stop me from wanting to know how she was holding up. She had just had my seed so I knew she was worried about the baby and my stepson.

Whenever Detective Tate and his sidekick walked out leaving me alone in the room, I noticed how my heart rate sped up. I started to pray and hoped I wouldn't get slammed for knocking off the nurse. *What the fuck else could this little interrogation be about?* I knew Emilio was a man of his word. *He'd kept it solid about everything else so why bullshit me on the charges being dropped? The nigga had fronted me a hundred keys before so what could his motive be? Was it because I owed him money? Damn, could it be the shit that happened between Margaret and me?* Emilio had never led me to believe he knew anything had ever transpired between the two of us. Speaking of Margaret, I needed to contact her too. I didn't even know if she was really pregnant, and if she was, did she have a *son* or *daughter* for me? If so, I had to get my kid because it was clear the chick was unstable. I wasn't heartless, so if there really was a child I would be a father to mine.

Yeah, that shit had to be his motive. Shit had to be a setup. I had to think if I was Emilio and wore his shoes I wouldn't let a muthafucka break my daughters heart I would surely put the nigga who caused her pain six feet deep because it is my job to protect her heart.

Cache

I WAS ALREADY SICK OF THAT BALL-BUSTING prick Fernandez and he hadn't been in there longer than five minutes. First of all, them bitches decided to leave me locked up in the cold-ass interrogation room for about three hours before coming to do whatever the fuck it is they'd come for. That shit ain't do nothing but make me mad as hell. I knew it was one of the scare tactics used to get the accused to confess to a crime, but just like it didn't work the first time, it wasn't happening this time either. I had no clue what we were in this bitch getting questioned for, but I needed this shit to be over like yesterday.

I wasn't worried at all about the crime I'd committed on Jusiah. Tony told me that shit had been taken care of and there was no reason not to believe him, especially since the shit had been broadcasted all on the news, Facebook, and everywhere else on social media. Somebody had definitely been arrested, and they had also confessed to both of the murder charges they were trying to pin against Tony and me. So the question remained, what the fuck could all this bullshit be about? *CO? Fuck! Could this be what the fuck all this was about?* I thought I had dotted all my i's and crossed every t.

Before my mind could proceed with any further thoughts, in walked Detective Tate as if his presence would be a blessing to me.

"Listen," I slammed both open palms on the table in frustration. "I want my fuckin' lawyer," I said, "I don't have shit to say. If you had anything on me or my man, I wouldn't be sitting here in this cold ass room for hours being questioned about some dumb shit. I have no clue what you talking about!"

I'd had enough of that shit. The detectives had questioned me for hours and I still refused to confess to some garbage-ass murder charge. Even if they'd claimed to have enough evidence to convict me and throw my ass on death row, I still wouldn't have had shit to say. I stood up and walked to the door.

"Am I under arrest, Officer?" I asked politely, purposely not referring to them as detectives. *Fuck these pigs,* I thought. I was prepared to walk out that bitch if they wasn't going to charge me with anything. I knew my fuckin' rights.

"Alright, suit yourself. If that's how you wanna do this ... you're under arrest for the murder of Carnel Price ..."

After I heard my brother's name, anything else the detective said had been drowned out. There was no fuckin' way I was really getting arrested for the murder of my own brother. At any moment, I was expecting Ashton Rutcher to jump out with a camera crew with big smiles plastered across their faces. But as the silver bracelets, that weighed a ton, were being placed around my wrists, I knew that shit was really happening. At that very moment, there wasn't a damn thing amusing about what was happening to me and I was no longer the brave and fearless bitch I had just been seconds prior.

*What the fuck is really going on?* My thoughts were running wild, and I was too shocked to even say anything or speak up for myself. It was a bullshit-ass murder charge and them two punk-ass detectives knew that shit.

"My own fuckin' brother? What the fuck?" I finally managed to say aloud.

"We've seen worse, my love," he said, jerking my arms. "Let's go." *Not where I'm from*, I thought, *only white people do dumb shit like that*. We might have Black-on-Black crimes galore, but to kill my own brother? Shit just didn't add up, primarily, because I was, and had always believed in being *"my brother's keeper."*

*Did Tony help CO kill my brother?* I thought. That was the only explanation I could come up with. The shit was hitting too close to home. Plus, shit was just too sweet between us to be true. Good things didn't happen for bitches like me. Here I was, head all in the clouds behind that fool, like shit was all gravy. A wolf in sheep's clothing. It only made my mind wonder as to the true motives behind Tony placing a ring on my finger in such a rush. *Was it stilla law that I didn't have to testify against him because of our marital status? Not that I would be, but had he married me for insurance just to be sure?*

My mind raced a hundred miles an hour trying to figure the shit out as I waited in the East Baton Rouge Parish Jail once again for a murder charge I hadn't cosigned. You would've thought I would've learned the first go 'round but it seemed that this revolving door was inevitable.

## CHAPTER 2
### CACHE

Hours later, I had finally been given permission to leave the Parish Prison. I didn't have to call a ride—my favorite girls were outside waiting with extended open arms, literally. As we closed in the space between us, me, Chanel, and Klimax, fell into one another's arms instantly. Releasing all the pain that rested on my soul, I cried as they embraced me. I cried because I couldn't wrap my mind around any of it. I couldn't understand the bullshit that was going on or *why* it was happening to me. I just didn't get it. Was God that angry with me? I thought the Word said "He would never put more on you than you could bear."

They say at the end of every storm you'd be greeted by a beautiful rainbow. Well, there I was still waiting to see it. In my world, rainbows were only an illusion—a myth. Why the fuck had I been dealt this ugly ass hand? It seemed as if everyone I had ever opened my heart up to and allowed myself to love, always seemed to betray me in some way or another.

This time around though, the Devil had really earned his place in hell, because in my eyes, my little brother could do no wrong, and neither could A'nett. *When will this storm be over?* The more I thought about everything that had occurred in my life, the more I believed the theory that there were just some things you would never get the answers to. What was God trying to tell me? Or was it the beast himself? Lucifer spared nothing or no one when he came to steal, kill, and destroy.

The Devil knew how to hit you where it hurt and if you let him, he'd demolish you—chew you up and spit you out like a piece of gum. You had to be strong and not fall victim to becoming his playground, but I wasn't strong enough to turn the other cheek, and by all means, this last game he'd played was the straw that broke the camel's back. In that moment I felt my transformation, and any sense of love, peace of mind or sense of stability was alleviated. For me, all humanity was gone; it had departed as if the rest of the "good" inside me had crossed to the other side.

After we released one another from our tightly-gripped embrace, the three of us got inside my new car—the car Tony had just gifted me as a token of his love. When I got inside, that "new-car" smell hit me in abundance, and the smell became one I hated because it reminded me of him. It turned my stomach. Everything that ever symbolized good for us, now symbolized bad. The thought made me recall a book I'd read by the author Adrienne. I understood her, because "When A Good Girl Goes Bad," the Devil himself couldn't stop the shit I had brewing.

I let my girl, Chanel, drive. I just wasn't in the right mind frame to get behind the wheel, so I hopped my ass in the backseat. No need to stunt like I was stable enough to function because I wasn't. The shit that was happening was enough to send a bitch straight to a mental home.

Caught up in my thoughts during the entire ride, I sat silently in the backseat. I needed a distraction, anything that would keep me from the hideous thoughts I was having. I must've really been deep in my head because when I looked up we were at the house—the house Tony and I had shared.

I looked over to the side of me and realized I couldn't recall when we had stopped and picked my kids up, but I know we had since they were sitting right next to me. Khasir was the first to hop out before grabbing A'miracle's diaper bag. He was always willing to help me in any way he could. He was every bit of his father, and some woman was gonna be proud when he called her "ma" one day. I was gonna make sure my son knew the correct way a man was supposed to treat his woman and that he'd know how to pick out a diamond instead of a phony. I knew there were women out there who would try their hands with him, but he would know when the fight was worth the war.

"Momma, let me open the door for you," Khasir said, once he got out of the car. He ran to my door to open it even though I stayed on him about running. I had always been too afraid he would fall and hurt himself and I didn't want my baby doing that, but today I gave him a pass.

Once we had all made it inside no one said a word—not even Khasir. He had gone back to being a kid again instead of my protector. I watched him as he played Fortnite and my baby loved that damn game. I couldn't stop my mind as it drifted to his father, and without warning, a tear escaped from my eye. I still hadn't told Chanel or Klimax what Tony and I had been arrested for. I knew I would soon have to, but I didn't even know where to start.

Honestly, I was still confused my fuckin' self. I tried ignoring the elephant that sat in the middle of the floor. I knew Chanel wanted to pry but she didn't want to overstep her boundaries. If she only knew. I couldn't answer any of it myself, so I did what I knew how to do best … avoided it. Of course, I wanted to believe he wouldn't do this, but the evidence was there. What was his fuckin' prints doing on the gun? Hopefully, he could explain all of this better than I could.

I headed to my room so I could change clothes because they smelled like the Parish Prison. Afterwards, I grabbed my purse and keys and headed out the door. I was running from my problems even though I knew running wouldn't solve the shit I had to face. At least getting out of the house for a little while would help me clear my head. Right now, I was in my feelings, but it wouldn't be long before my mind drifted back to homicide.

With no true destination in mind I decided to just get in my car and drive. I didn't even think to notify my sister or Klimax of my departure. They knew to keep an eye on my babies because they could tell I wasn't in the right state of mind to do so. I knew they understood. I wasn't ready to relieve my soul with what happened back in the interrogation room and if I stayed any longer that's exactly what would've happened. She was gone flip once the truth came out and things would surely get ugly. I could see the shit now ... She would definitely point the finger at me as if I would ever hurt any of them.

*Carmel and Chanel are twins, I meant 'were' twins*, I thought, catching myself. Out of the four of us, the two of them had always been closest. *How the fuck was I going to explain this shit?* I thought again. I should have never gone running my ass back to Tony in the first place. I should have left well enough alone but that's what happened when love called, or had I been associating love with lust?

C.R.E.A.M had always been a motivator for me, and even though I knew money was the root of all evil I had always basked in its glory. I took a chance on the nigga and he fucked the game up heavily.

I had lived on the dark side for many years. I'd participated in many robberies, left people for dead, sold drugs, and I'd done drugs. A straight up rebel, I really lived a violent life. Kevin Gates couldn't have said the words written on the tablet of my heart any better: "Might not notice but I'm strapped, bitch act a ass. I gotta cook 'em." The shit Tony had pulled was unforgivable.

As my eyes traveled from the road to the rearview mirror, all I could see was straight darkness in the window to my soul.

## C.R.E.A.M. 3

I remembered seeing one other person that lost that flicker of light, Ann. Growing up I had tried but couldn't understand what had happened to my mom along the way. I couldn't understand her way of thinking, but as I progressed through life, I started to get it. It was like some of us were put on this earth to go through things in order to have a story to tell, but I wasn't feeling this story. It was time for me to become the muthafuckin' director of this movie because that's exactly what my life was feeling like. Maybe it was a dream, and if that was the case, I was waiting to be pinched so I could wake up from this horrible episode.

Damn, how could I be so stupid? Tony was just like every other no-good-ass man I had ever run across. I hadn't even completely healed from poppin' out the nigga's seed and here it was I'd found out he'd had a hand in my brother's death. I just hoped this nigga knew I was my brother's keeper and I wouldn't stop until he paid the piper. Just when I thought I could put my wicked ways to rest, he'd made me realize they had only been put on the back burner, and now, the pot had begun to boil over. They say pressure will burst pipes, or better yet, will make you bust a nigga's head instead.

Proverbs 14:1 reads: "A wise woman builds her home, but a foolish woman tears it down with her own hands." Call me a fool, but I was definitely here for destruction and it was time to double down.

Yolanda Moore

## CHAPTER 3
### TONY

*Damn*, was all I could think as I walked what some refer to as the "Green Mile." I had already been dressed-out which meant I had exchanged my street clothes for the bitch-ass orange jumpsuit and brown shower slippers. As I walked down the breezeway with the intake bag thrown over my shoulder, I could feel niggas' eyes on me. I wouldn't dare fold, so I kept my head held high as if I was the king of the jungle, but little did them niggas know, they could have that shit.

"A yo', Slim?" I heard a familiar voice yell out to me, but I didn't pay the nigga the attention he was looking for. For one, the name was Anthony a.k.a Tony not *Slim*. So whoever the nigga was would've done better pitching rocks through the ocean if he thought he was gonna gett a reaction out of me.

As I continued to G-walk, my mind was on one thing and one thing only—using the fuckin' phone to call Cache. I needed to speak to bae like last year, fuck yesterday. A nigga could hardly breathe with the fact of knowing my baby was fucked up behind all of this. I could feel it in my heart and the separation was real. I just hoped and prayed she would give me a chance to explain. I hadn't touched no one in a while and there was only one fuckin' explanation. The night the cops were speaking of I had let CO pull the wool over my eyes, and the nigga had really blindsided me with what he'd done. This shit wasn't just about Cache, nah, not at all. Even from the muthafuckin' grave the nigga was causing havoc.

"Yo, Killa, what's the bidness?" I heard a voice say, as soon as I stepped onto the tier. I didn't have to play the guessing game to see who it was beckoning for a nigga. There was only one muthafucka in my entire life who called me *Killa*.

"Muthafuckin' D, my muthafuckin' nigga!" I said, smiling for the first time in a while as we G-hugged and slapped hands with opposite arms swung over each other's shoulder. "Damn, nigga, this where the fuck you been?" I asked, as we pulled apart from our embrace.

"Shit'd, my ass been in this bitch, but you know they can't hold a real nigga down long. I heard you the man with the plan, tho'."

"Nah, I'm just a squirrel tryna get a nut."

"Come on, my nigga, we need to have a sit down."

"Right now I gotta call my girl, I'm tryna shake and bake, my nigga," I said, as I proceeded to walk to the phone station with one thing on my mind.

"My nigga you might be the king of the streets but I'm the king of the jungle." He smiled as he threw his arm over my shoulder. I made a quick interference though. I bent down to pick up my intake bag.

I had known D all my life, but I didn't need none of them bitch niggas thinking shit was sweet. I knew how niggas got down behind the wall and I wasn't that nigga. I wasn't with that homo shit, and forgive me if I was wrong, but I hadn't seen or talked to my nigga in a while. I honestly didn't know what the fuck he meant about "being the king of the jungle" and I wasn't trying to stick around that bitch to find out either.

I knew he'd caught my drift, but he didn't seem to take offense to it. My nigga or not, he knew my truth, and he didn't waste his breath calling me *Killa* just for bustin' ass on XBOX either. D knew I didn't mind laying a nigga at the feet of Christ and I knew he didn't either, so keeping that thought in mind, I knew I needed to keep my enemies close and my friends closer—you know, just in case a nigga so happened to get lost in the system.

## C.R.E.A.M. 3

I ended up following the nigga anyway instead of going to the phones. I wanted to see what the fuck he wanted that was more important than me calling home. As we approached D's cell block, I could feel the off-brand ass niggas checking me. I guess, to see who the new nigga on the block was. I wasn't even trippin' though, because real gone recognize real. If them niggas couldn't respect who I was, I definitely had a chip on my shoulder and I was ready for a nigga to make the wrong move. *Right about now I'm coming straight from the "I-wish-a-nigga-would foundation" just to earn my stripes*, I thought. Whoever dared to fuck with me was surely to cure my appetite because the beast inside of me was blood thirsty.

"A yo. I got some shit in this bitch that none of these niggas can't even dream about unless they come through me," D said, as we stepped into his two-man cell. It was clear he'd turned it into his own personal man cave. He had his cell strapped with everything—a TV, a microwave, and a small fridge like the ones used in college dorms—the muthafucka even had a game system.

"You in this bitch living penitentiary rich, huh?" I asked, still standing at the gate checking his shit out. No way we were at a real prison.

"Fuckin' right. I wouldn't want it no other way, especially knowing it's a possibility a nigga might not never see the other side of the world again," he said, shaking his head. My face froze with a questionable look as if to say: '*nigga, speak for yourself.*'

"Tony, I know what you thinking, mane. Like, a nigga don't got no hope. In a sense, a nigga really don't. You know this system was created by the White man for niggas like you and me, ya feel me?" *Did this nigga really have the nerve to ask me some bullshit like that?* "I'm just saying, this shit just modern-day slavery," he added.

"Fuck no, I don't feel you. I'm not tryna spend the rest of my life in a cubical-sized cell. I'm tryna make something shake. I'm not tryna be penitentiary rich. No offense, but I just had my first child. A little girl. ... A'miracle and she needs me so fuck all of that shit," I said, getting emotional just from the thought of losing my daughter. "Look, I do need to go make a few phone calls though so I'ma holla at you later, my nigga," I said, tossing my intake bag over my shoulder.

"Hold up, my G. That's my purpose for this here reunion," D said. He turned around and headed toward the toilet in his cell that sat right next to his bed. He leaned down to cut off the water on the toilet before removing the stainless steel top, where you flush. I couldn't really see everything he had inside it because his body blocked my view. However, I didn't have to wonder long because once he put the top back on, he walked over to me with a brown paper bag and placed it in my hand as if I'd just made a quick stop at the gas station.

"Aye, don't look inside the bag now but once you get in your cell you good."

"A'ight, good looking out my nigga." We G-hugged once again before I turned around and headed to the phone to call my wife.

Cache

WITHOUT EVEN REALIZING I had a destination, I ended up at Hall Davis and Son Burial Site. Carmel, A'nett, and Ann were all at rest, but what I wasn't sure of was if they were at peace with the way things had turned out. I wondered if my mother and siblings were turning over in their graves. For starters, Tony and I had been living a lie and he had snaked me the whole time. I had been so blinded by the fuck shit, I had a baby for his ass. I knew I had to make the shit right because everything was all fucked up. My loyalty had always been to my family, and I felt like I had let them all down.

As I took a seat in front of their final resting places, my mind started flashing back to the good and bad times we'd had. Now, to me, the bad didn't matter, because if I could go back, at least we would have each other and I wouldn't be sitting here buried in pain. I would at least still be able to hug them, kiss them, and even beat they ass for fuckin' off in school or some shit. Mane, how I would give up a kidney just to see Ann's crooked smile or give my life just so they could live and not get caught up in my shit.

"Lord! Woman, you were truly a force to be reckoned with. You lived your life how you wanted, did what you wanted to do, and dared any bitch to fuck with you, huh, Ma?" I spoke out loud, really wishing she could hear me. I knew if Ann could respond back she would say some crazy shit like: *'fuckin' right I'ma live my life how I want, and it ain't a bitch on God's green earth gon' tell me how to live it!'* The thought made me laugh because I could hear my mother's words as if she was right there in front of me.

*"Cache,"* I heard my brother say next, in the tiny little voice he spoke in when we were kids.

*"What, brother?"* I would respond back as if I was annoyed because that was the shit big sisters were supposed to do when their lil' brother called.

*"When I get big, shit's gonna get better for us, just watch. I'ma man up just like our daddy and take care of my family."*

The memories of our pasts hit me hard, and a tear dropped from my eyes as Carnel's voice faded from my thoughts. I smiled as I recalled the way he had always poke his chest out whenever he talked about protecting his family. As I wiped the tear from my smile, I touched his headstone with the same hand, hoping he could somehow feel the pain my heart bled for him. Fuck, it was the same pain I was gonna let niggas feel for taking him away.

My phone started ringing and brought me out of the murderous thoughts I'd started to conjure up. I looked down at the lit screen and saw it was a number I didn't want to answer—a 1-800, nope. I hit ignore and kept it pushing—no need to answer calls from unknown numbers or bill collectors.

Needing something to calm my nerves, I remembered seeing a rolled blunt in my ashtray so I decided to go get it. I really didn't smoke, but under the circumstances, I felt like Bad Azz. Chanel and Klimax had to be the ones guilty of leaving it. Besides that, I was still on fuckin' parole, but right about now, my mind was saying fuck everything and everybody—Parole officer included.

As soon as I was back at my family's gravesite, I didn't waste any time lighting it up. I took a position and leaned on my brother's headstone, with one leg extended out flatly on the ground and the other bent at the knee. When I inhaled the smoke I watched the cherry on the end come alive. And again, my thoughts were, *fuck it, fuck parole,* I told myself smiling. For what, I didn't know, maybe it was the weed 'cause the shit really had a bitch feeling good. Not even a good five minutes had gone by since my first toke and I felt my eyelids start to get heavy. My body started to crave that familiar feeling. Once a weed head, always a weed head. I guess there was no such thing as quitting. One thing I could bet my life on though was that I would never go back to the days of hustling in the clubs and fuckin' with hard drugs to take away all my demons. *I shouldn't have been fuckin' with that bullshit from the jump,* I thought and shook my head.

That bitch One was the fuckin' devil who wears Prada. The bitch was definitely reincarnated, and I didn't want shit to do with her. There was only one way we could make amends

... she had to go. On some real shit, I was so fuckin' disappointed in myself for not putting the bitch in her eternal resting place. All I had to say about that was the bitch had better count her blessings since the good Lord had spared her life so far. When the time came and we were face to face, I would be the one to walk away. I made a promise that I'd be the person who would stop that bitch's clock from tickin'.

"What's good, lil ma, you okay?" I heard a deep voice behind me. I couldn't tell who it belonged to and I had fucked over too many not to be aware of my surroundings. I quickly wiped my tear-stained face and tried to erase all evidence of the pain I felt. However, not even the act of drying my eyes could take away the glooming expression that rested upon me.

"Yeah, I'm good, but the last time I checked, this was the perfect place to cry and not be judged or questioned about it. I mean, after all, I'm surrounded by the dead," I said, trying to make light of the situation and not show the ugly expression I knew was written all over my face. That was just something I could never change about myself. I always wore my feelings on my sleeve. *Damn, he looks familiar*, I thought.

"My bad, love." He threw his hands up as if he didn't mean any harm and I knew he hadn't. I was just being a bitch and wasn't in the mood to be fucked with is all.

"It's fine," I said, waving him off, letting my cold exterior melt away. "You good," I continued. For the first time I noticed I had let the blunt go out. Before I could re-light it though, the muthafucka took a seat beside me and grabbed the weed and the lighter as if I had invited him to have a seat. *Fuck it*, I thought shaking my head. Deep down I welcomed the distraction, and might I add, one hell of a hot distraction.

"I'm Latray but everyone calls me Tray for short." That was all he offered and I didn't pry for more either. I assumed he'd gotten his swag from the streets, and like every hood bitch, I was addicted to niggas like him.

"I'm Cache," I said, introducing myself as well. Maybe it was because I was lonelier than a muthafucka and needed the company of someone who didn't know the troubles I held close to my heart. Who knows? Maybe I needed his company but was afraid to admit it. Or it could've been because when I looked up at his sexy, brown-skin ass he turned me on and had me squirming on the inside. I might've been down and depressed, but my pussy had a beat of its own.

I shook my head at myself knowing it was very inappropriate of me to have wanted to ride his face right among the dead. I could feel my pussy cream, but I wouldn't tell a soul ... not that there was many around. Instead, I just took the blunt from Tray and pushed the thoughts of having his pretty juicy lips on my swollen gushy pussy, out of my mind ... for the moment anyway.

# CHAPTER 4
## TONY

I was every fuckin' bit of heated. I was beyond mad! I had no understanding as to why Cache's fuckin' ass wasn't picking up her phone. Call me selfish, but I didn't have time for her ungrateful, spoiled ass to be on the bullshit she was on. I knew she had to be grieving all over again, but it wasn't like I knew it was her brother Carnel at the other end of my gun when I pulled the fuckin' trigger.

"Fuck!" I said aloud, and slammed the phone down for what seemed like the hundredth time.

I grabbed my intake bag and headed to my cell, trying to hold my head up. I couldn't lie, the shit was hard like a muthafucka but I refused to let them niggas in there have something to call home about. Shit, Ca$h couldn't have said it better when he wrote that book "Thugs Cry."

The first thing I noticed when I walked into the box assigned to me was that I would be bunking with another muthafucka. I had really been hoping I would have my own space.

"Ain't this some shit," I said under my breath. I didn't know who my cellmate was and there wasn't anything around this bitch that gave the shit away either—no pictures or nothing. I guess I was about to earn my strips around there because I wasn't the type of muthafucka who wanted to sleep on top of another nigga. So, I took it upon myself to move the nigga's shit from the bottom bunk to the top.

After moving the flimsy ass mat onto the empty top bunk, I placed my state issued property on the bottom bunk and took a seat on the bed, I prepared myself mentally for whoever walked through the entrance. I didn't even waste my time removing anything from the bags just in case I ended up having to pack my shit to go to the hole.

Ten minutes had passed and so far no one had made the grand appearance I had been patiently anticipating. I decided to come out of beast mode and came down a notch, but I continued to lurk so I would be ready just in case a nigga tried me.

Just as I started to relax, as best as I could under the circumstances, my mind fell on the bag that D had given me back at his domain. *What could I possibly need that would be in a bag?* I wondered to myself. Curiosity was getting the best of me, so I decided to go with my move to put my mind at ease. Before looking inside, I walked to the entrance of the cell to make sure the coast was clear. The same shit that had been going on earlier was still in motion so I was good. Niggas were in the dayroom either playing cards, watching the basketball game because they were gambling, or they were watching Jerry Springer. Damn, the same shit niggas swore not to do at home they were definitely doing in there. Who did that?

After walking back inside the cell, I began to unravel the brown paper bag. I peeked inside first before just placing my hand inside of it. The first thing I noticed was another brown bag had been wrapped around itself tightly with tape so its contents would remain inside. I picked it up, opened the bag, and was surprised to see a few grams of dope. Also written on the outside of the bag was a number for a cash app. I continued to go through the bag and came across a throw away phone, a shank made from a piece of metal which had been sharpened enough to cut through a steak, and wrapped around the end was a handle made out of tape—the kind you would see in a doctor's office—there were also some cigarettes and a BIC lighter.

To be honest, the only thing I was excited to see was the phone. I needed out of this place, and even though I appreciated the nigga D coming through for me, damn … What he thought a nigga was gonna be there for a while?

"Hello?" I heard my nigga Terrance say through the ear piece, sounding like he'd just woke up. "Who the fuck this is?"

"Nigga this muthafuckin' Tony!" I said, getting aggravated

"Damn, nigga, my bad. I didn't know the number. What's good, big homie?"

"Look, I need you to come through for a nigga."

"Aight, nigga, run that shit. You wasting time, give me a name," Terrance said, ready and willing. The nigga had just got out of Angola a couple years prior so this street shit was something small to a giant. The nigga also didn't mind dying, so I made a mental note to double down on more niggas with his attitude about life.

"Nah, it's nothing like that yet but I need you to see what's up with my girl and why she ain't answering the fuckin' phone."

"Aight, I got you, my nigga, as soon as I get down to the bottom of this I'ma hit you up."

"Aight, cool. And as soon as these cracker bitches set one, I might need you to touch this bond too." With that said, I ended the call. Nothing else needed to be said, and as for Cache, her muthafuckin' ass was gone make me fuck her world clean up. I had let her get away with too much shit and now the shit was coming back to bite me in the ass. I tried calling her a few more times but I still wasn't I' no fuckin' answer. I sat on the bunk for at least thirty minutes. "Fuck it," I finally said and tried one last time.

On my last attempt a big Kool-Aid smile plastered across my face because I had finally gotten through, but my smile quickly turned upside down. Without me even getting a *hello* in I could tell the phone had been answered by mistake. A pocket call. I couldn't actually hear exactly what was being said or going on but as sure as my mother named me Antonio Clark my bitch was with some nigga who was clearly comforting her as she cried. I didn't know who it could've been because the only other man in her life besides me was her brother Carnel. And since he was dead there was no way it could've possibly have been him, and even if he wasn't he definitely didn't go by the name Sixnine. Trigga was right, smartphones start shit!

Right at that moment, my mind started going a hundred miles per minute. I didn't know anyone by that name but I was surely going to find out.

"A yo, Tony, you good, my nigga?" I looked up as D stood in the doorway. I knew I was slipping because I hadn't even heard the nigga walk up.

"Yeah, nigga, I'm good. I just need to get out this bitch, before I go crazy and just start killing niggas 'round this bitch, dawg." D laughed as if I had told a joke, but joking was the last thing on my mind. The same things that made you laugh would also make you cry.

"Let's go hit the yard, my nigga," he suggested. And since I knew sitting in that cell wouldn't get me nowhere except death row, I followed him.

\*\*\*

"CLARK, GET DRESSED. You got a bail hearing!" one of the correctional officers yelled. I instantly perked up being that it was four o'clock in the morning. I had been waiting patiently for that day to come. If the judge granted me a bond I was getting the fuck out of there, no questions asked.

After thirty minutes of getting ready and waiting for the officers arrival, I was cuffed and escorted down to the holding cell as they were issuing breakfast. You would think after being in that bitch for thirty days a nigga would've been hungry enough to at least try the shit but not me. I wasn't fuckin' with it. One thing I didn't like was for a nigga to cook my food, especially in prison. Them muthafuckas wasn't to be trusted. Plus, I'd heard all kinda rumors and I wasn't tryna see if they were true or not, fuck that. Don't get me wrong, a nigga needed something to survive off of so I had copped out to bread and water. I had also placed a workout into my daily intake but wasn't sure how much longer I was going to be able to live off that alone. I was for sure ready to survive off the land if I had to do prison time.

I looked around the holding cell and took in my surroundings 'cause you never knew who, or what, you would run into. Stepping inside, I walked straight to the back of the cell and stood with my back against the wall. I didn't trust any of them niggas and I needed to make sure I could see any and everything moving in that bitch. Prison reminded me of 'survival of the fittest,' and if I had any say, I would definitely be a survivor.

"A yo, Tony, what's good, my nigga?" I heard someone say from the right of me. It took me a second or two to spot who the voice belonged to.

"What up?" I said, once my eyes landed on the nigga who had called my name as if we shot marbles.

"Damn, nigga, why the cold shoulder?" I looked at the nigga like he was crazy. Dawg you don't remember me do you?" I still didn't answer. "Boy, we were locked up together last time you were in this bitch."

"Bruh, you got the wrong one. I'm not that nigga," I said, wishing the lil Kevin Hart look-alike would get the picture and get the fuck out my face. It was too damn early for a nigga to be talking especially if his ass ain't brushed his teeth.

"Nah, bruh I'm sho'—

"Listen, get the fuck out my face before I smash yo shit."

"Look, 'nough said my brother," his lil short ass said. With his hands in the air, he walked backwards and accidentally stepped on a few nigga's toes. "My bad, my brother," he told the dude who was sleeping on the floor with his arms tucked inside of his orange jumpsuit. If looks could kill this muthafucka would be dead already but I'ma let nature run its course because dude laid on the floor looked as if he had been running the streets hard and was happy he was finally getting some rest. At about seven o'clock the door was opened, and the people aka officers began calling the names from the court docket. I listened closely until I heard my name called for the second time that morning.

"Clark," I heard over the hustle-and-bustle of the courthouse noise. I stood and walked through the crowded-ass holding tank, bumping into muthafuckas on my way out. A nigga was definitely being treated like an animal and I didn't like the shit one bit. Along with everyone else, I finally made it into the hallway to get the restraints placed back on me.

Once everyone was restrained in cuffs and shackles, we were escorted to the transportation van in a line. The shit was straight bullshit and it reminded me of a slave camp. If you asked me, racism was still alive. The white man continued to be the owner and the jailhouse was the plantation. The one thing I know for certain ... *if I have to do time I ain't workin' in the kitchen or on the yard pickin' grass, and I damn sho' ain't workin' cleanin' no muthafuckin' toilets niggas done sat they nasty asses all up on,* I thought, as I walked passed a nigga in a trustee prison outfit. *The bitch might as well put on a skirt, but I ain't about to kiss a muthafucka ass just for them bitches to hold shit over my head. Nigga, I'ma be good or good at it, straight like that. I will not be forced into submission.*

## C.R.E.A.M. 3

The ride to the court house was short-lived and we made it to our destination at 8:45 a.m. on the dot. That was good since court started at 9:00, so we had made good timing. As soon as I stepped inside the courthouse I was immediately taken to the courtroom. I looked around at the audience to see if I spotted a familiar face. To my surprise, Cache was there with Khasir, my stepson, and my baby girl looking as beautiful as the first day I'd laid my eyes on her. My heart instantly slapped a beat which traveled right down to my dick making it jump. *Damn,* I thought, *she looking good.* I imagined rubbing my hands over her curves as I licked my lips the way she liked me to. Just looking at her made a nigga feel proud, as if I had hit the lottery. Then, some bitch-ass nigga with dreads sitting beside her showed the ultimate disrespect by placing his arm around my bitch. We locked eyes for what seemed like an eternity, and if looks could kill, we would've been two dead muthafuckas. Cache's ass had some nerves showing up with that clown-ass nigga on my court date. Her ass was on some straight up shit.

"All rise!" the bailiff said, interrupting my killer thoughts as the judge stepped out of his chambers and into the courtroom. We all stood up. "The Honorable Judge Richardson presiding."

"Thank you. Please be seated." Judge Richardson took his seat first as we followed.

"The state calls Antonio Clark to the podium." That was my que to stand in front of the mic.

"Could you please state your name, date of birth, and place of residence for the record?" Judge Richardson asked.

"Yes, sir. Antonio Clark, D$^{ec}$. 19th, 1990. 400 Spanish Town Drive, "I spoke into the mic and stepped back once I had finished speaking.

45

"Mr. Clark has been indicted on a first degree murder charge for a Mr. Carnell Price. It is State's wish that Mr. Antonio be denied the bond hearing that he and his defense attorney is asking for today."

As the charges were read I wished Cache hadn't been there. I knew it had to hurt her hearing the charges being read out loud in open court. But now it made sense why she had come in the first place, and it wasn't to support me, that's for sure. If only she would've given me the chance to explain what happened that night.

"Your Honor, the motion that the State is trying to get denied has not even been filed, but we would like to file an oral motion to have bail set. It is clear that the District Attorney's office has already tried and convicted Mr. Clark before he's even had a fair shot."

"Your Honor, the accused has been charged with first degree which is a capital offense. He is a threat to the community."

"Your Honor, the State is lacking evidence against my client and the little that they think they have will not stand up at trial. Could I approach?" my lawyer asked, holding a folder up in her hand.

"Yes, you may but make it quick. I've got a full docket and plan to get through it today." *Damn, this muthafucka don't play, huh?* I thought to myself.

Once my lawyer approached the bench the folder was immediately handed over to Judge Richardson. As he took a look over the paperwork, I tried reading his expression but to no avail. For at least twenty seconds he looked over the paperwork. "Did you get this?" The question was directed towards the D.A.

"Yes, Your Honor, and Mr. Corey is deceased."

"So, why does it look as if you are wasting my time? I need both of you to meet me in my chambers. Court in recess! We'll resume in ten minutes."

"All rise!"

"Damn, that muthafucka look madder than a hoe with a wet ass who got robbed for some pussy," one of the niggas on that court docket said.

Once the Judge, the D.A., and my fine ass attorney walked into the judge's chamber, some of the people in the audience conversed while others walked out to do whatever it is they needed to do before the ten minutes were up. I couldn't help but glance over at Cache. That hoe really had me ten shades of fucked up if she thought I was just gone lay flat and let that shit slide. *Fuck all that!*

As soon as I started to formulate a plan to fuck both they asses up, court was back in session.

"Mr. Clark, after thoroughly going over your file I've decided to set bail. If you wish to make bail I will see you in six months to start trial. You are to stay out of any trouble. If you engage in any illegal activity I will not hesitate to lock you up and throw away the key. Mr. Clark, do you understand me, son?"

"Yes, sir. Thank you, Your Honor," I said, as I stood in front of the muthafucka, despising the fact that my life was in his hands. For now, I'd play by his rules. I needed to get out that bitch like yesterday and that was my only concern.

"Don't thank me now, because you may not have a reason to later down the line," he said gravely.

As soon as I got back to the prison I called my lil baby, Desire. She had been riding for a nigga heavy and her actions made me wonder why I even wasted my time with Cache, but of course, we always wanted what we couldn't have.

Yolanda Moore

# CHAPTER 5
## CACHE

After leaving the courthouse, I was heated that bail had been set for the two-timing muthafucka I once considered my man. Here it was finally coming to the light that I had been sleeping with the enemy the whole time. *How could I betray my own flesh and blood? There is absolutely nothing in the world I could do to avenge his death except draw blood*, I thought, as I sat in the passenger seat of my car while Tray navigated through the streets.

"You good?" he asked, placing his hand on my left thigh.

"Yeah," I said. I lied since I definitely wasn't in the mood to answer rhetorical questions. Why the fuck would he ask me some stupid shit like that? Who in the fuck would be in their right mind finding out the person they loved, had a child with, and would lay their life on the line for had killed someone else who meant more?"

"I'm not the enemy, love," he said, and wiped the tears that I didn't even know were falling, from my face." Whatever you need me to do, I'll do it no questions asked. Your pain is my pain, and I'll lay a whole muthafuckin' nation at your feet just to see a smile on your pretty face. Never forget that," he said, reading my mind. The fact that I was the absolute wrong bitch to fuck with must've been written all over my face and it must've showed in my body language, but his touch and carefully spoken words slowly melted the ice off my heart.

"Are you sure?" I asked, though there was only one correct answer.

"No doubt. Just say the word and nothing else is required." *Alright*, I thought, as I continued to look out the window. *No hesitation detected*. My mind began to spin as I thought of a master plan. I mentally formulated a hit list and Maya was the first bitch on it. There wasn't anything in the world that could stop me from slitting her throat and ripping her heart out.

Once we pulled up to my house, I grabbed my baby girl and headed to the front door with one thing on my mind ... *murder*. I knew exactly what needed to be done in order for that bitch come out of hiding and show her face. Without saying a word to Tray, I headed straight to A'miracle's room, placed her in her playpen, and packed her a bag. After grabbing everything I thought she would need, I headed to my room where Tray had laid across the bed, remote in hand without a care in the world. I stepped inside my walk-in closet and for just a second, admired all the things that only money could buy. Everything Tony had ever bought me wasn't because he loved me. He had only been trying to make up and fill the void he had been responsible for all along.

Coming out of my trance, I grabbed my two Coach suitcases. I peeked over my shoulder to make sure Tray hadn't stepped inside with me. Once I saw the coast was clear, I went to the safe Tony kept loaded with cash and started stuffing as much money as I could. By the time I finished, I had four bags overflowing and I was ready to go.

"Where you going?" Tray asked, still laying in the same position I had left him in.

"I got some business I need to handle," I said, walking out the door to put the bags in my car. I grabbed my keys on my way out. I popped the locks and threw the bags in the trunk just as fast as I had thrown the money inside the suitcases. I looked up just as Tray stood at the door.

"What you mean?" I thought we were in this together?"

"Trust me," I said, walking past him, keeping my keys close. *I would hate to have to lay this muthafucka down all because he on some hoe shit, trying to get me to stay,* I thought.

"Trust you? How the fuck am I supposed to trust you when I don't even know what the hell is goin' on or where you goin'!" he shouted. He followed me as I walked into my master bedroom and relieved myself of my clothes to take a quick shower.

"I don't have time for this. If all you want to do is argue, you got the wrong bitch, and I'm telling you now, I'm not in the arguing mood. Now if you would let me shower in peace," I said, standing in front of him just as naked as the day I was born.

"Don't have time, huh? I should have known this bitch ass shit was gonna happen. Here it is you sitting here playing the fuckin' victim. What? You been waiting on that nigga to make bond? You gone fuck that nigga?" he asked, grabbing me by my neck. "Bitch, if you think it'll be that easy for you to just walk away from me you got another muthafuckin' thing comin'." He looked at me with his face scrunched and his jaws clenched.

For a minute, the nigga had turned into the devil right before my eyes and there was absolutely nothing I could do about it. *Damn! Why the fuck I always run into the crazy muthafuckers.* If I didn't know any better, I would have thought he was a nigga from my past who had some kinda fuckin' vendetta against me. He grabbed a handful of my hair and yanked my head backwards with so much force, I swear it gave me whiplash.

He started kissing on my neck and I can't lie the shit turned my ass all the way on. It had been months since I had been touched, and quite frankly, I was sexually frustrated which is why I had been snappy. I had been so fuckin' stressed out due to all of the shit that had been going on in my life. I had been asking God to remove all the bullshit out of my picture frame, but it seemed like the more I prayed, the stronger the devil attacked. It seemed like every time shit started to become sweet, everything would quickly go south like I was just not supposed to be happy in this lifetime. *Maybe the next*, I thought. I let my mind follow my body because right at that moment, the bitch was betraying the fuck out of me. My juices had begun to flow in overtime and I could feel the shit rolling down between my thighs.

"I'm the head nigga in charge! Fuck that pussy-ass nigga, you hear me, huh? Do you understand what the fuck I'm saying to you?" He shook my neck as he took a handful of my pussy and started playing with my clit.

"Mmmm, Latray, fuck..." Sounds of pleasure slipped from my mouth involuntarily, letting his bitch ass know I had started to like the pain as much as I liked the pleasure. However much pressure he applied to my throat, he matched it by applying the same amount of friction to my clit. When I caught a glimpse of my reflection in the full-length mirror of the bathroom, I realized I had become very flushed.

"Aaaaah! Fuccck, I'm about to cum!" I screamed so loud, I could only hope the neighbors hadn't heard me. My pussy had exploded right in the palm of his hand. If his hand had been a bucket it would've definitely overflowed. My legs began to shake uncontrollably, and if it hadn't been for Tray picking my weak ass up and placing me on the bathroom's countertop, I would've fallen right where I stood. Never in my life had I cum so hard from a nigga just playing in my pussy. The shit made me wonder *was it love or lust* (in my Kendrick Lamar voice). Either that or a bitch needed to be slapped and choked more often.

He stuck his hand inside of his pocket and pulled out a Trojan and his dick all at one time. Either the nigga had my head spinning causing me to see twice as much dick, or the muthafucka was really blessed with a supa-sized penis that had a pretty brown mushroom top. He approached me as he stroked his rock-hard dick, ready to beat my insides and turn them to tenderized meat. Watching him climb on the counter with me had me confused since I was ready to be fucked. Besides, I had already made up my mind that I was still leaving after it was all said and done, and I didn't see shit wrong with it—niggas did it all the time.

"Come on, lil momma, climb on top and ride this dick like your life depends on it," he said. And if I didn't know any better, I would've taken the nigga serious, but then again, who knew. His meat stood at attention, long and strong. The head thumped like it had a heartbeat, and as if it had a mind of its own, my clit thumped in parallel and perfect sync. I climbed on top, legs still shaking from my orgasm. I lowered myself and allowed him to enter my slippery passageway, and he filled me up to capacity.

"Fuckin' right. You know how long I been waiting to feel this good shit? Huh, bitch?"

It could've just been that I was tripping, but I couldn't help but wonder what the fuck he'd meant by the statement he'd just made. I mean, in all honesty, I had just met the fool. I let the shit slide though because I didn't care how good my pussy was. I wasn't in the position to talk shit and his ass wasn't in the right state of mind for me to just pop off as if shit was sweet.

Tray held my waist as I grinded my hips into his, making him hit every spot inside my tunnel as if he knew me inside-out, in that order, I could feel another nut coming so I began to speed up, creating my own rhythm as my pussy began to contract on his dick. I could feel my nectar coming down like a thunder shower.

"Uh, uh, uh, I'm fuckin' cummin'," I moaned, as I made the ugliest face. I knew I had because of the mirrors on the counter that I was face to face with. As I watched myself bounce up and down, up and down, on his pole my tits bounced too, and the shit turned me on like no other. I don't think I had ever been fucked like that before.

"Aaah, fuck! Here, ma, take that dick," he yelled, as he erupted inside of me. "That shit was good, love, now get up and let's get in the shower together," he said, as if shit was sweet.

\*\*\*

THE NEXT MORNING ROLLED around fast as fuck and even though I was still completely dick-matized, I was on a mission and didn't allow the shit to pull me away from the task at hand. I rolled out of the bed trying my best not to wake his wacky ass up. As soon as my feet graced the plush carpet, I quickly moved around, throwing on clothes, and grabbing the things I hadn't had the chance to grab the day before due the unexpected fuck fest.

I looked around mine and Tony's room one last time before placing my hand on the door knob and turning it.

"Where the fuck you going?" I heard Tray say from behind me. I swear if I had to shit I would've done it right on myself. I turned around to look at his crazy, good-dick slanging ass and decided in that moment that there was no reason for me to lie. I mean, how the hell could I? I had literally got caught red handed, leaving with my bags in tow.

"I don't-don't want to argue with you but I can't stay here," I said, hearing myself plea.

"Bitch, you can't be serious. You still want that nigga, don't you? What more do he gotta do to you before you realize the nigga don't love you?"

## C.R.E.A.M. 3

Damn, his ass just didn't get it. I had shit to do and sitting there going back and forth with his ass just wasn't working. I discreetly slid my available hand in my tote bag and placed my hand on my gun to give myself a sense of security. I was not about to let what happened the night before happened again, and get in the way of what I had to do. If I hadn't given in and gave his ass some, it would've been curtains for me, so I couldn't let that happen again.

"You might not have been the one who pulled the trigger on your brother but you just as fuckin' guilty." Before the bitch nigga could say anything else I pulled my Draco on his ass with the quickness.

"Get the fuck out of my muthafuckin' presence you insecure ass bitch before *'I am'* the one to pull the trigger," I said. My hands shook but not out of fear, but the fact that the bitch had pushed a button I usually don't allow bitches to push.

"So this is what it's come to, huh?" he asked, slightly stepping back, throwing his hands up.

"Bitch, I said get the fuck out. You know my muthafuckin' rep. I ain't scared to splatter your fuckin' brains all over this bedroom wall like I'm Picasso. I done turned plenty of walls into muthafuckin' canvases. So try me."

"You know what, ma? I'm not even gonna charge that to your heart 'cause I know you, and I also know you hurtin'. But know this, I ain't never let a nigga or bitch point a gun at me and live to talk about it, so let that be your warning. Don't try that shit again. I'ma let you cool off. I'll be around when you need me, ma, and remember, I'm not the fuckin' enemy." He slowly backed out of the bedroom. I watched until I couldn't see him anymore. I stood there, still pointing my gun, just in case he had a change of mind.

Finally, I heard the door slam. I hadn't even realized I was holding my breath. Once I came back to, I ran to A'miracle's room to check on my baby girl. She was still in her crib sound asleep. I then ran to the front door and looked outside. Just as I looked toward the way I knew he always left, I spotted his car turning the corner. *Good. I'm happy he made the decision to leave in peace instead of in a body bag.* At that moment and the way I was feeling, it wouldn't have made a difference which road he chose to take.

Once I noticed the coast was clear, I continued with what needed to be done and got the fuck out of dodge. Next, I sent my sister a text message to let her know I was enroute.

Tony

I WAS HAPPIER THAN A MUTHAFUCKA to finally be a free man and to breathe fresh air. As I stepped out of the prison community I just stood there taking everything in that I had once taken for granted. Never again. I would die before I went back to that bitch.

*Beep! Beep!* I looked up in the direction of someone blowing the horn. At first I didn't know it was for me until I saw D'zyna step her sexy ass out of the car. I knew none of my niggas would come up to personally pick me up. Niggas hated the jailhouse and we avoided it at all costs. So trust me when I say I understood to the fullest. Without saying a word, I got into the passenger seat. She pulled off into traffic without so much as a glance.

I only had one thing on my mind and fuckin' was the furthest thing from it. D'zyna was definitely a good girl but I was married and just didn't have that type of time to spare. I promised to call her later in life but right now I had too big of a plate to pile any more on to it. So, after dropping me off at the crib, I headed straight inside. The first thing I noticed was Cache's car was missing from the driveway. I could honestly say that was to be expected. It wasn't like I got jammed for killing some random ass nigga. It was her own flesh and blood. A nigga just needed time to explain the facts, but with the disappearing act she'd pulled, wasn't no telling if I'd be granted the chance to do so.

When I walked inside the house I instantly felt the emptiness. I headed straight to the kid's room, and of course, I got the same results—nothing. I took a seat in the rocking chair and remembered the last time my wife and daughter had sat in that very same spot. Clutching my hands together and holding my head down was the absolute only thing I had the strength to do. I couldn't remember the last time a nigga had to pray, but if no other time had mattered, this one surely did. I knew I had fucked up.

After all the shit I had been through with that woman, I just refused to believe she could wash her hands of me and not grant me the chance to speak my peace. I got up from the chair and my next stop was our bedroom. I headed straight for the walk-in closet we shared. The first thing that grabbed my attention was her luggage wasn't where she always kept it. As a matter of fact, all of her luggage was gone. Realizing that made me take a quick inventory of her clothes and shoes. It seemed as if everything was still accounted for. That conclusion led me to believe there could only be one explanation for the missing luggage—*my money*! I headed straight for the safe and there was no reason for me to go any further. The door was cracked open, and I could clearly see she had cleared it out. I opened the door completely and noticed my gun was also gone. But what I did see was a piece of paper she had left behind. Grabbing it, I immediately began to read what she had written:

> Tony, by the time you get this letter I will be long gone. There is no reason for you to look for me because there will be no

words spoken. With that said, I do have a bullet with your name on it, and if you want it just as bad as I want to give it to you, then I suggest you should go with your move. I have cleaned every stash that I know you had. So, no, unlike you, I'm not going to slither on my stomach and leave you wondering and trying to fill in the blanks. They have already been filled for you. Fuck you, and I hope you receive every fuckin' thing in life that hurts, including missing what we've created. I know my baby will be just fine. Look at me without a father. Men only complicate things and you are no different from the rest. Have a nice muthafuckin' life.
                    Sincerely your wife, #C.R.E.A.M

All the fuckin' money in the world wouldn't be enough to mend the pain the letter had caused. The money she had taken was the furthest thing from my mind, plus I had plenty more where that came from. If Cache was any other plain-Jane-ass bitch I would have ordered a hit, and by nightfall, she would've been wearing a toe tag, but she wasn't. She was my muthafuckin' baby momma, my wife, and as fucked up as it may have sounded, I need my girl back.

I took a deep breath and gathered my thoughts. If Cache had gone that far to leave, I knew it wouldn't make any sense for me to call her phone. But since none of it made any sense, I dialed her number anyway. *Just what I had figured, straight to voicemail.*

Next, I dialed the next best option, Chanel.

"Hello?" she sounded as if she had just woken up.

"Don't hang up. Please don't."

"Boy, you got some fuckin' nerve callin' my fuckin' phone," she yelled.

"Listen, everything ain't what it seems. You know how much I love your sister and I would do anything for her."

"Including lie, so get off my damn line."

# C.R.E.A.M. 3

"No, wait, Chanel. All I'm asking is for you to hear me out. You know I'd never do anything to jeopardize my relationship with Cache. You gotta believe me," I said, as the phone went silent. "Hello," I said, making sure she was still there.

"I'm here, but I'm not the one you should be pleading with. I can't fuck with you, and if I ever see you, I don't know how shit will end. And please don't doubt me, 'cause if you make one false move, I'll be the first to show you that Cache ain't the only muthafucka who gets down with the devil." With that said, she hung up in my face. I wasn't worried about the threat. Not saying I was taking what she'd said lightly because there wasn't nothing I wouldn't put past a muthafucka with the last name Price.

Yolanda Moore

## CHAPTER 6
### MAYA

Only a few people knew I was back in town—my precious grandmother and my favorite cousin. The bitch was my ride or die. I was back to my mischievous ways which was why I decided to show my face again. Not that I had taken a break, because a bitch was always making calculated moves. I played Chess not Checkers, which is why the opposition couldn't keep up with the moves I made. Cache had to step her game up to fuck with a bitch like me.

Before I made any move though, first I needed to pay my respect to A'nett. I dropped some fresh flowers off and talked to her. I let her know how sorry I was for not protecting her from all the shit she'd endured, which included things that happened before I knew her. I could relate as a child and that was exactly why I am the way I am today. I didn't give a fuck who you were, I didn't give passes. The streets made me.

After I left the gravesite, I headed to my cousin's house. She stayed in Broadmoor Plaza Apartments, which to me was a good thing, because no one knew me back there and I was trying to stay under the radar.

"Hey, girl, how are you?" she asked, hugging me as soon as she opened the door. "Come in," she said, coming out of our embrace. She stepped to the side so I could enter inside.

"What's that smell, D? Bitch, I know you not in this bitch cooking girl?" I laughed, as I headed straight to the kitchen. Her ass couldn't cook.

"Nah, bitch you know a hoe like me will never be domesticated. I ordered some shit through Uber Eats. I know you gotta be starving. The food just got here so it should still be edible."

"That's what's up," I said. After washing my hands, I grabbed the bag of food from the table. We headed to the living room to get comfortable on the couch before digging in and going for what we know.

"So ... what's up with that little business I asked you to handle?" I asked, not wanting to waste any more time on small talk.

"All work no play, huh?" she asked, laughing.

"Come on now, bitch. If nobody knows how I'm rocking, bitch you should know me like the back of your hand," I said, speaking the truth.

"Of course." She smiled. "Well, Tony is a hard nut shell to crack. The nigga not as easy a target as we thought. Pussy definitely ain't his main course, unless it's coming from that hoe, Cache." No lie, when she said that shit, it put a bitch in their feelings and I didn't like it one bit. I had to find a way to get at that nigga.

"What else can you tell me?" I asked with my attention fully on her. If I was a dog, my ears would've been standing at attention and my tail would've been wagging.

"Well, let me finish with Tony first. After losing the nigga for the lil time he was locked up, I bonded him out like you told me to. I let him believe his homeboys had sent me. I definitely proved to be the Bonnie to his Clyde, but he still tossed me to the side like yesterday's trash."

"Bitch, you should've had the nigga hooked by now! What the fuck?" I said agitated.

"Listen, hoe, don't question my womanhood. I got this. It's just gonna take a little longer than I thought." She rolled her eyes.

"D'zyna, listen sweety, don't play any games I know you bitch, so next time you see that nigga, I want a bullet in the nigga's head. I know the nigga is a charmer but bitch we the foundation to Charm school."

"Really, bitch?" she asked, right in the middle of chewing her food.

"Yeah, really, and don't talk with your mouth full 'cause grandmother taught us better than that. So what about Cache? Any report on her?" I asked, anxious to know what had been going on in her world.

"I'm glad you asked," she said, as she stood up and walked back into the kitchen. Two minutes later, she came out with some Champagne glasses and a big gold bottle of Ace of Spades. I swear the girl put *drama* in *dramatic*. I watched as she filled the glasses. She passed me mine.

"What's the celebration?" I asked.

"Well, before you ask, *no*, I don't know where your girl took off to… But what I do know is who she been spending time with while her nigga was locked up."

Now the bitch had my attention. "Who?" I asked curiously.

"Damn, bitch let me take a breath. A nigga name Tray."

"Who is he?" I asked with my face scrunched unknowingly. The name didn't ring a bell.

"Now that's the million dollar question because its apparent Cache has no clue she jumped out of the bed with one enemy into the bed of another one. Do you remember Tony's friend CO? The one the streets saying Cache killed?" I responded by nodding my head *yes* urging her to continue. "Well, Tray is CO's little brother," she said, handing me an envelope.

"Well, I'm trying to put this shit together," I said out loud.

"No worries, big cousin, I already did that for you," she said smiling. "They were fuckin' with each other after Tony got slammed. But after court, I followed them back to Cache's place. I decided to sit out there a little while because my gut told me some shit was about to pop off. I just knew the bitch wasn't bold enough to just have the nigga laid up in Tony's crib, knowing his bond would be set."

*If only she knew Cache*, I thought. "Watch ya mouth," I said, letting her know I was the only one allowed to call Cache out of her name, just like I was gonna be the one to kill that hoe if she didn't get with my program. No lie, I was past putting up with her fuckin' mind games.

"Look, cuzzo, you know I'm team you all day long, but just like you not that bitch, neither am I. Our blood flows thicker and longer than pussy juice and don't forget that shit. So don't forget what side of the fence I'm on. With that being said, I formulated a plan that would eliminate the rivalry starting with this bitch," she said, as she spread the pictures of Cache and Tray on the table.

"Now we talking my kinda language. What's the plan?" I asked.

For the next few hours we set everything in motion because we were going to execute our plan before the day was over.

Latray

IT HAD BEEN HOURS SINCE I'D LEFT Cache and she was seconds away from blowing a nigga's head off. I would be lying if I said the shit didn't turn me on like a muthafucka, but I would also be lying if I said I was gonna let her ass live after pulling out on me. As I sat and had flashbacks, all I could think about was how she'd left my brother laid out in the road like he wasn't loved. Thank God I had sense enough not to let her ass know where I laid my head, because I was sure she'd thought about what I'd said. The worst thing she could have done was allow me to walk out of that house.

# C.R.E.A.M. 3

Over the few weeks I had been fuckin' with ole girl and getting to know her, I had stared to relax which was why I wasn't strapped. I had more than one agenda and that was why I hadn't left her ass pushing daisies a long time ago. I wanted to play her at her own game and rob the bitch. Ever since my brother had been gone the dope game had dried up and ends had been hard to meet. My mom was losing her house because her son, my brother, wasn't here to foot the bill like he'd always done, and of course, my mom didn't have a stash put up for a rainy day. Fuck, she didn't expect her son to be there one day and gone the next, even though she knew the life he lived. A mother should never have to bury her children, but Cache made that possible for my mother, and the bitch had left me no choice but to do what I had to.

After losing my brother I went into a deep depression. I couldn't sleep or eat. My whole world had come crashing down on me all at once, especially knowing the muthafucka who killed him was still breathing. But so was I. It was a clear indication that I'd failed him. Straight facts, and to me that shit was heavy. If it was the last thing I did, I promised myself I would find the people responsible, and here I was. I was tired of hearing muthafuckas say, *'God's plan was this and God's plan was that'*. I couldn't understand "God's plan" and really didn't know if I wanted to understand His plan. I knew the kind of nigga my bro was and if the shoe was on the other foot he would've been stepping on muthafuckas for me with no questions asked. That's why I didn't give a fuck about who I had to touch in order for my brother to rest in peace.

The day I stumbled upon Cache had to be a nigga's lucky day. I had just got back in town and wanted to visit his gravesite. No lie, the shit felt stupid talking to a slab of granite, but for whatever reason, I felt a sense of peace. When I spotted Cache I didn't know who to give glory to because what I had in store for her wouldn't be pleasing in the eyes of the Lord. I didn't know if Cache knew it or not, but her survival skills had become a gift and a curse. She was a legend in the streets and all types of niggas wanted a piece of her because she had heart. The bitch was ice cold without even knowing it and that was exactly what made her perfect. She was a true queen, and she played the part with no effort. She didn't have to try to be a boss because she was, and niggas and hoes bowed down every time she blessed them with her presence. But see, this time, she had fucked with the wrong nigga.

She was the walking billboard for the saying: "Never Trust a Big Butt and a Smile'. She was like Robin Hood—she took from the rich and fed the poor. Those were all the things I'd heard, but you could believe none of what you heard and only half of what you saw. Hands down, the bitch had piqued my curiosity. There was something about her story that grabbed my attention. If we were in another life, she'd be mine.

"Babe," Jewel called out to me, and grabbed my attention from my thoughts.

"What's up?" I responded dryly, not wanting to be bothered.

"What's on your mind?" she asked sweetly. Her leg lay thrown over my hip and our legs entangled. She reached down and rubbed my stomach.

"Cache," I told her truthfully, but she didn't get it. She knew a nigga mind stayed on money and that was what she assumed now. *Money over everything.* I lived by it, and I was willing to die about it. I was married to the streets and no one in the world could come along and change my view on the way I thought.

Knowing how to turn me on, Jewel started kissing me on my neck, but pussy was the furthest thing from my mind.

## C.R.E.A.M. 3

Pussy was meant to be fucked, and no matter how good a bitch was in bed, I could never give her what she wanted. Like every other woman I knew, Jewel thought seduction would get her where she needed to be in life. Her expectations were too high and me and shawty wasn't even on that type of time. We lived two different lifestyles. In a perfect world she would be Clair Huxtable. But since the world we lived in wasn't perfect, I was still that nigga who loved the streets more than anything and anybody.

"Damn, you must have more than money on your mind."

"Why you say that?" I asked, playing along like I didn't know what she was referring to.

"Well, because ..." she whined, as she sat straight up in bed and pouted. I knew it was about to be some shit. Usually, you would be all over me fuckin' my brains out, but you're not. Another bitch must have your attention," she said. I wasn't sure if it was a question or statement.

"Mane, no cap, but you really trippin'," I said, laughing at her correctness. Shawty knew what was up without me even saying. She knew I couldn't give her what she wanted. That was something we'd established from the jump, so why trip now?

"Are you serious right now, Tray? I been here for you for years, *'no cap',"* she said, mocking me, "but I'm sick of your bullshit!" Ignoring her, I decided to roll my ass clean out of the bed because I knew she was about to start her bullshit—she did it once a week. I just shook my head and laughed. "Right now I don't find anything fuckin' funny!" she said. She slid right out of the bed with me.

As she walked behind me throwing question after question, I headed for the bathroom. I turned on the shower first, then stepped out of my boxers. I closed the door in her face not wanting to hear none of the bullshit she was pulling out of the side of her neck. She knew, under no other circumstances, would I have let any of that foul shit slide if she was any other bitch. Fuckin' with Jewel was something I'd always regretted. When my bro got killed I let my guard down, and now the bitch knew too much of my business, so I was stuck like Chuck until I found a way to free myself.

After closing the door on her, I guess she finally got the picture because I didn't hear her yelling from the other side any more. No lie, before she'd started blackmailing a nigga on some shit, I was feeling her ass. Then all the bullshit started, but that's another story for another time, 'cause settling down just wasn't in the equation for me. Due to the kind of life I lived, I wasn't promised to make it home by sunset, nor was I guaranteed to ever feel it shine on my face again. Who knew...

When I got out of the shower, she was nowhere in sight. *Good. Out of sight out of mind,* I thought. The solitude gave me time to mentally prepare myself for the day. I was headed out on the block to go fuck with my bro, Nic. It was early as a muthafucka, but the one thing I knew for sho was, niggas like me was always on it. *Money over everything.* Me and Nic were always on the everyday hustle-and-bustle. We didn't have time to beef with niggas and definitely didn't have room on the clock to pencil these hoes in. And again, fuck a nigga 'cause not only would I push a muthafucka's wig back for the right price, but I'd push that shit back for something as simple as trying my hand. There was nothing and no one who would ever be allowed to come between me and that bag. Experience had taught me if you let a nigga slide once they wouldn't be as easy to get rid of, and that was exactly why the muthafucka responsible for my brother's death had to go. No if's and's or but's about it. There wasn't shit that could be said or given to take the shit back and nothing would make me forgive and forget. Cache's life was the only thing that would be enough compensation. She had acceptably stood behind the gun and pulled the trigger, so I hoped she was ready to stand in front of mine.

Once I got fully dressed, it was time for me to hit the pavement. Just as I was headed out the door my phone start vibrating on my hip.

"Yo, tell me something good?" I said through the phone not bothering to check the caller I.D. I already knew exactly who it was—my nigga Nic. Not too many had my main line and the ones who did didn't have the courage to hit a nigga too early unless it was about money. Money talked and bullshit walked.

"Money is good, my nigga, that's what," he said. I could tell there was a big ass smile on the other end of my phone. What nigga didn't smile while speaking of money? Especially when the shit was good? The only time I had anything other than a smile on my face when talking about money, was when a nigga owed it to me.

"What's understood need not be explained," I responded back. "I was just headed out the door."

"Nigga don't tell me Jewel stayed over?" Nic asked, already knowing the answer.

"Of course," I said with false excitement in my voice," Nic already knew it was far from the truth.

"Look, my nigga, you already know I'm not about to do all that hoe-ass pillow talk and shit over the phone. I'ma catch you up on everything when I get there," I said, as I stepped out the door. I hung up the phone without giving him a chance to say anything else.

\*\*\*

FORTY FIVE MINUTES LATER, I had finally pulled up on my nigga. I knew he was gonna be pissed because it had taken me almost an hour to come through. I had to clear my mind and I also needed to formulate a plan to get at that bitch Cache. After thinking a while, I had come up with the perfect master plan. The more I thought about it, the more it made sense to me. The plan was to get at her, but the only thing I knew that would definitely set her off was to kidnap one of her kids. I could kill two birds with one stone. Make the bitch pay a ransom for them kids. She would turn the streets upside down to get the money for them lil muthafuckas, and then I could pay the nigga Mark back.

"A yo, my nigga, how long you been out here?" Bringing me out my thoughts, I turned to see Nic tapping on my window.

"Nigga, just hop in, bruh," I said, as I pulled on the blunt hard to fill my lungs.

"Was happenin', my nigga?" We slapped hands and embraced.

"Not a muthafuckin' thang that I don't want to happen," I said, passing the blunt.

"'Nough said, my nigga. So what's up with that bitch Jewel?"

"Dawg, fuck that bitch. A nigga really sick of all that mouthing the broad be doing.

"Yeah, no lie, the bitch be trippin'. The hoe was blowing my shit up like we fuckin' or some shit," he said laughing, "that's how I knew some shit was up." He laughed.

"Nigga ain't shit funny 'cause what I shoulda done when you introduced us was turned the bitch down like I do my collar. Nothing that comes from you is ever with good intention.

"Boy, you dumb," Nic said, shaking his head.

"Whatever, my nigga. Let's roll," I said. I pulled off and realized I had just formulated my plan. *There's only one way to go about getting back at that bitch,* I thought.

A devious smirk sat glued on my face.

Yolanda Moore

# CHAPTER 7
## CACHE

"Bitch, I need you to stop all that stupid ass stressing. You know the only way to get over a nigga is to replace his no good ass with another," Chanel said.

"Fuckin' right," Klimax chimed in. "I do the shit all the time. You know these niggas ain't loyal, so neither am I. Fuck that shit," Klimax said, pretending to pick dirt from under his nails.

"I don't know what the hell happened to you sis, but do I need to remind you that momma didn't name yo ass Cache for nothing, love. Now let me fix this bird nest on the top of your head 'cause you just letting yo self go, hoe."

"That's what's really giving your state of mind away. You can't keep saying you 'good' or 'okay' 'cause actions speak louder than words, honey," Chanel chimed in.

"It's written all over your face ... you don't have to say a wooord..." Klimax started singing as soon as Chanel exposed my ass.

"Bitch, I know you smell those musty ass armpits of yours 'cause I can. You got a bitch not even wanting to come to visit y'all hoes," Klimax said, as if I wasn't in the room.

"I'm sitting here you dick-suckin', cum-swallowin' bitch."

"Duh, don't you think we know that, Cache? I gotta give it to Klimax. We can smell your ass from one room to the next," Chanel said in agreement.

"OK, you know what? We about to start acting like the white folk and have an intervention," Klimax said excitedly.

"Bitch, niggas don't have interventions we just go with the flow," Chanel said.

"Y'all bitches act like I'm on fuckin' drugs or some shit. I'm not no damn junkie."

"Girl bye. You in this bitch looking and smelling like one. If nobody else know you know I do ... Even when we were kids and didn't have a pot to piss in and a window to throw it out of, bitch, you kept that kitty clean. I remember when you use to take hoe baths when momma couldn't keep the water on. Now a bitch can afford to buy out water works and you acting like you done lost your damn mind over some dick. Shake back, bitch.

"And girl you are withdrawing, it's called "lack of penetration". What happened to that fine ass nigga, Tray, I heard you been creeping with?" Klimax asked, simultaneously butting in and telling a bitch's business.

"Tray? Who the fuck is that?" Chanel looked at me all weird and shit.

I sighed. "Girl, nobody," I said, as thoughts of his good-dick-slanging-ass crossed my mind.

"So bitch you still being a hoe, huh?" Chanel asked.

"You can take a hoe out the hoe house, but you can never remove the hoe out of the whore, darling." We both looked toward Klimax and gave his ass the evil eye.

"Give me a break, bitches," I said, as I headed toward the bathroom. I closed the door behind me, looked in the mirror, and wasn't happy with what looked back at me. The truth? I was going through withdrawals from being away from Tony. *Is it safe for me to say I still love the nigga?* I thought. Looking back at my reflection, I was too afraid to even say Tony's name aloud.

"Yeah, we gone give you a break alright as soon as you shake back, queen. While you been in this bitch on a depressed quest, not only have the kids lost they no good ass pa, but if you don't get it together, they gonna lose you too. So get ya shit together, bitch," Klimax yelled outside the bathroom door.

"Shake back, Cache," I said aloud to myself as I splashed water on my face. I looked to my left and noticed my phone sitting on the countertop. I must've left it in there. I couldn't remember the last time I'd seen it. That was how cloudy my mind had been. I picked it up to see if I had any missed calls or text messages. I had more than a few. Some calls were from Tony, Knowledges' parents number as well that meant my baby must have called. Yeah, I'm fuckin' up. *I ain't never not told them goodnight*, I thought, shaking my head.

I had dropped them off a few weeks ago and hadn't been staying at the house. In fact, I didn't have the desire to ever step foot back in that bitch.

I took a deep breath and decided right then and there I was taking back control of my life. I ran some bath water and soaked in the tub for about forty minutes, cleansing my body and my thoughts.

As soon as I stepped back into the room with my support system, I was ready for the world. I decided to say fuck it and let my hair down, if only for a little while.

"You know what? Fuck it, I'ma go out with you hoes even though I know you bitches wanna use me up," I said, laughing because I'd always accepted my big sister duties with no problem.

"Bitch, please. Yo name might be Cache but mine is Chanel, so momma ain't just stop pushing out gold diggers when she had you. All my niggas take care of me too, so let tonight be on me."

"Hold the front door!" Klimax yelled. "And see that's exactly why both of you bitches my best friends."

"Girl, nobody ain't said shit about you. Besides, you been creeping enough lately ... suckin' dick and poppin' pussy, so you should be buying my ass a drink. Yo ass already late on your half of the bills."

"Girl, I know damn well you ain't expose me in front of the queen? I carry my weight in these streets just like the two of you bitches, if not better. But, hold up, let me get you these lil measly ass dollars," Klimax said. Rolling his neck, he reached his hand inside his bra to retrieve his money for his half of the bills.

"Y'all bitches crazy, and every time I come over here y'all remind me why I don't do roommates. If I'ma shack up with somebody it's gonna be a nigga with a stiff one, 'cause his ass gone be up in everything in that bitch, including my guts and the back of my throat. Ain't nothing gone be short changed about him."

"You right, sis. I just can't get rid of this hoe," Chanel said, snatching the money from Klimax.

"Oh it's nothing! If you want a bitch gone just open them dick suckers, and within a snap of them crusty ass fingers of yours, I'll disappear like that white hoe with the ponytail who keeps a bottle."

"Bitch, and who might that be?" Chanel asked

"Jeannie in a bottle. I'll disappear like my ass was never here," Klimax said, getting all emotional and shit.

"Come on now, bitch ... get the fuck on with all that emotional ass shit. You know a bitch would never put you out. Damn, I ain't never seen a man so gotdamn sensitive." We all laughed because in Chanel's eyes, all niggas were sensitive to her mean ass. I can say hands down that's the one thing she got from Ann's ass.

*Later on that night...*

## C.R.E.A.M. 3

After we were all dolled up, it was time to roll. I had dropped by to see my babies at my in-laws before heading out to paint the town red. Yes, no matter what or who I was doing, Knowledge's parents would always have that title, because not only did they love Knasir, but they loved and treated A'miracle as if she was one of their own.

"Y'all hoes ready to roll?" Klimax asked, as soon as I walked through the door. He dabbed his lips with gloss. "Just know if we take my car we ain't gone be rolling for long."

"Why?" I asked, knowing he was about to say some bullshit.

"Bitch, because I only put a dolla' and seventy-five cents worth of gas in my tank. A bitch clearly ain't living as lavishly as you hoes. Well, let me be forward. Cache I'm tryna roll in the Audi not the Honda," Klimax said.

"I know that's right," Chanel high-fived Klimax.

"You hoes is childish," I said, "neither one of you bitches got a Honda and gas is two thirty a gallon so I know you didn't put a dolla' nothin' in your tank. But we can roll in my shit," I said, tossing Klimax the keys instead of Chanel this time.

"Bitch, our shit might as well be Hondas. Who else can ride in a car designed in a year that ain't even come to pass, beside a bitch like you?" Chanel asked

"Alright, you win bitch. Let's go," I said, as we walked out the door. We hopped in my car and pulled off into the night.

"Did Chanel tell you our secret code name for you?" Klimax asked smiling

"What is it ? Please tell me. Is it High Class Hooka? I know that's what you bitches think of me, but we all know it ain't trickin' less you got it."

"Nah, baby girl, it's much more juicier than that. Come on Cache you should know a bitch know you better than that now"

"OK, what is it?"

"First 48." Klimax and Chanel laughed.

"You hand-me-down hoes need to stop." I joined into their laughter.

"*Hand-me-down*? No she didn't! I would say that pussy is hand-me-down but I never had any of that good shit. But I *can* be the judge of them bundles looking like fundles."

"No, baby, you the only one that got glue to the scalp. Cache and I were blessed with tresses. Thank you very much, ball head bitch," Chanel said, before I could switch sides.

"Let's talk about something else. One thing my momma taught me was under no circumstances, never discuss ya life insurance, ya dick, and definitely not ya weave. So, moving on." We laughed as I drove down the road.

"I thought you would see things my way," Chanel said. I swear the both of them hoes needed a check the first, third, and the fifth. I smirked and shook my head.

"Fuckin' right, bitch. Shit, two out of the three already got snatched from my ass. The dick, and a bitch been letting niggas snatch the weave! And you should have been able to figure out what the two were, honey. Plus, let's just say my life insurance is still active." Again, the three of us burst out laughing. I swear Klimax could get a spot on the stage at Apollo.

\*\*\*

"A'IGHT, HOMIE, JUST name the time and place," Nic said. We crushed the streets smoking blunt after blunt since we worked better under the circumstances. Moneybagg Yo's *Code Red* album blasted through the speakers.

"Shit, tonight the night we make our move. We ain't got time to waste. Besides, I got the location on the bitch and her kids right now," I said, referring to Cache.

"Word?" Nic asked. He couldn't believe I was really serious about snatching her bad ass kids. Still, he was down for whatever I was ready to do. He knew how important my brother had been to me.

I had always lived by the "no woman, no kids" policy but of course Cache had been the exception to the rule. The bitch was the devil, and everyone knew the devil would use you in ways you never thought possible. He would have you going against everything you have ever stood for. The day I left her house, I had placed a tracker on her car as well as her phone, so the bitch had no clue I'd been keeping up with her whereabouts. I knew she had been by her ex-in-laws' house to drop the kids off, and I also knew she'd been staying at her sister Chanel's house.

She still had no clue who I was, and the dumb bitch thought we had bumped into each other by chance. Little did she know, she was in for a rude awakening. The day she pulled the trigger on CO, she might as well have turned the gun on herself and her whole family because her time was ticking.

"Boy, a nigga would hate to be on yo shit list. You a cold ass muthafucka to fuck a bitch the way you did, now you ready to blow her brains out. That's cold," Nic said. As he talked, he shook his head laughing at nothing, but everything. I could tell the effects of the weed had kicked in long ago.

"Yeah, that's the same shit my old bird been tellin' me all my life, so tell me something I don't know, nigga," I said in a serious tone. I pulled out my phone and looked at the screen. There were two blinking dots on a map that represented Cache's current whereabouts. "Oh yeah?" I said out loud and questionably.

"What's goodie, my dude?" Nic asked.

"This hoe at the club tonight," I said. Just thinking about how bitches hopped from one dick to the next in a blink of an eye tripped me out. I shook my head, lowkey frustrated.

"She got over you quick, nigga. You must not be laying pipe like you claim," Nic said laughing.

"Nigga, ask ya momma how good I lay the pipe."

"Boy, don't play with my momma, play with yo bitch."

"Whatever. You better be lucky I got more pressing issues to deal with otherwise yo ass and yo brains would be splattered on that glass for that bullshit you be spittin'.

\*\*\*

IT HADN'T EVEN BEEN TWO FULL HOURS before Nic and I were pulling up at Cache's in-laws' crib out in Denham Springs, LA. To be on the safe side, I dialed Cache's phone to make sure she was where the monitor indicated her to be. It would just be my luck that the bitch's phone coincidentally got stolen or some shit and she caught me slippin'.

"Hellll-o …" I heard someone answer the phone but knew it wasn't Cache. Even though I knew the voice wasn't hers, I couldn't tell who the fuck it belonged to. The loud music playing in the background answered any uncertainty I may have had about her being at the club.

"May I speak with Cache?" I asked to see what would happen.

"Yeah, could you hold, please?" I knew the person on the other end of the phone was lit because her words had come out slurred.

"Yeah, who is this?" I heard Cache answer, and immediately, a smile spread across my face for the first time in a long time.

"Checkmate, bitch." I hung up in her face leaving her to wonder what I meant.

"A yo, you bitch ass nigga! Wake yo funky ass up!" Nic threw a Popeyes Chicken fountain drink on the junkie whose car we'd decided to use. "Why you bring this bomb ass nigga with us any damn way?" Nic asked, as Cook jumped from the cold drink which blew his high.

Me or Nic said a word as we sat outside in the parked car. We checked our Draco's to make sure they were locked and loaded. We smacked the magazines back into the bottom of our guns and cocked the slides.

*Click-Clack!*
*Click-Clack!*

Next, we stepped outside of the getaway car, but not before pulling our ski-masks down.

"Keep the car running," I told Cook as he took my place in the driver's seat. I wasn't even sure who the nigga was but I guess it didn't matter. The only thing the nigga was concerned with was the fat ass crack rock he was promised at the end of his job.

"Yo this the spot?" Nic asked.

"Nah, nigga, we hopping out right here but we gonna run across town to get there," I said sarcastically while shaking my head. "Yeah, nigga, now let's go," I replied.

"You sure you can trust ole boy?" he asked, and nodded his head in Cook's direction.

"No, my nigga, not at all. And to be honest, I'm not sure how much I'm trusting you right now."

"Then why the fuck you asked the nigga to do the job with us?"

"Damn, nigga why so many questions?" I asked, somewhat irritated. "But to answer your question so you can shut the fuck up, I'ma slump his ass when we through, and if you keep asking dumb ass questions I'ma consider leaving your ass sleep right next to the nigga."

"Nigga, let's just go," he said trailing behind me.

"Now you talking my language," I said, as we made our way across the freshly-cut lawn.

Once we'd made it to the front door, I looked at Nic just as he signaled for me to go around back while he waited at the door. We had done this shit many times, so I already knew the routine and what was expected of me and vice versa.

Hopping over the locked wooden fence to the backyard entrance was the least of my worries. The patio had sliding glass doors that allowed me to see straight through to the inside of the house. And of course, they were unlocked. I don't know why niggas who decided to move out of the hood thought the suburbs were any safer. Them be the first muthafuckers not to put blinds up, acting like a nigga who ain't never had shit.

I entered the nice laid crib and let my eyes briefly scan the I. *Shit can't get no better than this,* I thought, as I closed the sliding doors quietly and slowly so I wouldn't wake up the sleeping house.

"Who the fuck are you and what the hell you doing in my damn—

"*Psst! Psst!* Firing two shots to the dome quickly, pops never got the chance to finish his sentence.

"Fuck," I said under my breath. I had to move quickly. *I definitely didn't come here for this bullshit,* I thought. I hurried my ass to the front door to let Nic in.

"Nigga, we got to move fast. I already had to lay one nigga down."

"Damn, nigga, already?"

"Yeah, muthafucka must've got thirsty and came down for a glass of milk or some shit. I don't know."

"Baby, is everything OK?" I heard a little old voice say from the stairway. The shit made me whip my head in that direction. Nic too, but he was the one to shoot.

"Oh my God," she yelled and took off running back up the stairs.

"Fuck, I missed!" Nic yelled. We ran in the direction the old bird had run.

"Get the bitch but don't kill her!" I yelled. I do a lot of shit in these streets but killing a nigga grandma wasn't one of them.

She had just made it inside a room just as we'd made it to the top of the stairs after taking them two and three at a time. Not having much time to secure the door, I kicked the bitch in just in time.

"I got this room! Check the rest of the muthafuckin' house!" I yelled towards Nic. "Bitch, is there anyone else in this bitch?" I asked, spitting all over the place. "And before you decide to lie, choose your words wisely, hoe!" I said aggressively. I wanted her to know we hadn't gone there to play patty cake.

"Yeeesss, my two grandbabies and my husband. Is he gonna be alright?" she cried.

"That's all up to you," I told her, lying through my teeth. I took the rope out of my back pocket and grabbed her by her hair to show I meant business. "Let's go." We walked back down the stairs to the kitchen so I could bind her to a chair.

"Please don't kill me," she pleaded for her life. I didn't say shit. I just continued with the task at hand. Once I was finished strapping her to the chair, I grabbed a kitchen rag and stuffed that bitch deep inside her mouth. Not wanting to turn the lights on, I walked around the kitchen blindly. I started rummaging through the kitchen drawers in search of some tape, and to my surprise, I didn't have to look long. Right there, in the top draw, was a roll of duct tape. *Bingo!*

"What's going on?" I heard Knasir ask as Nic escorted him and his sister down stairs. "Grandma, are you okay?" he asked again, rubbing his sleepy eyes.

"Mmmmh," she answered as best as she could.

"Take him to the living room," I said, not wanting him to fully wake up and realize what was going on. "Listen, I'm not going to hurt you but I'm taking A'miracle with me. I need you to deliver a message to their mother for me, okay?" She shook her head *yes* as her tears rolled freely down her face. If I didn't know any better, I'd have thought I saw her sigh when I told her I wasn't going to take 'her' grandson, and A'miracle would be going instead. Damn, that was cold. "One last thing … tell Cache everything ain't always as it seems and every smoke screen ain't a smoke screen. She always told me I looked familiar. She should have done her homework. If she thought CO was out there by himself the bitch thought wrong. Tell her she got the game fucked up 'cause I'll die and go to hell or jail, and take a "L" behind mine," I said with my mouth pushed close grandma's ear, making sure she heard the message I needed her to pass on.

When I walked in the living room Nic's ass was sitting in the recliner with A'miracle laid across his chest asleep, and Knasir lay next to him asleep as well.

"Let's go. Our work here is done. Leave the boy 'cause we did enough damage to this family but bring the girl. I wanna cause havoc with her bitch ass daddy. That nigga gotta see me."

# CHAPTER 8
## CACHE

The next morning after the club, I found myself laid across Chanel's bed. Every piece of clothing I'd had on the night before was missing. I lay there for a while not even able to open my eyes. My head felt like someone had put a shotgun to it and blew it off, except it was still attached to my body. I tried playing back the events of the night but couldn't remember exactly what happened. For whatever reason, I kept having flashes of Tony and I having hot-and-heavy sex. I could even smell the nigga's cologne.

"Damn a bitch got it bad," I mumbled. Then, taking me by surprise, I felt a heavy ass arm being thrown over me. "Bitch, get yo damn arm off me," I told Chanel. "Bitch, we not kids no more." I reached out to remove her arm but as soon as I touched it, I knew it was definitely not my sister's arm. *God, please don't tell me I was so fucked up last night I can't even remember bringing a nigga back here with me, and Lord forbid I gave the nigga some.*

I slowly opened one of my eyes to see exactly who it was. And boy was I surprised. "What the fuck are you doing in the bed with me!" I screamed and jumped up like fire was under my ass. I went straight for Chanel's nightstand and grabbed the gun I knew she kept there just in case— and this was definitely a *just-in-case* situation.

Woah. What the fuck you doing?" Tony jumped up just as fast as I had. He threw his hands up in surrender causing his big dick to sling everywhere.

"*What the fuck am I doing*? No muthafucka, the question is what the hell are *you* doing? Did you fuck me last night?" I asked. I was heated because I already knew the answer to the question. That was exactly why I hated clubs and alcohol; a bitch was liable to do any damn thing, and this was one of those *do-any-damn-thing* moments. "I'm really hating myself right now," I said.

"Cache, please just hear me out. That nigga CO set me up.

"Bitch, what the fuck is going on in this muthafucka!" Chanel and Klimax burst in the room, swinging the door open like mad women.

"Chanel, I was just trying to explain to your sister what I explained to y'all last night." I swung the gun toward Chanel and Klimax.

"What the fuck is he talking about? Somebody better open they muthafuckin' mouth and I mean quick before I start dropping bodies in this bitch," I said, still feeling the effects of the liquor from the night before.

"Cache, just put the gun down and we'll explain."

"Bitch, what? Y'all in cahoots or some shit?"

"Now bitch you going too far! You know muthafuckin' well if the nigga ain't have evidence to prove he wasn't guilty, none of us would be standing here right now. I would've definitely set this scene up like a murder-suicide." I thought about what Chanel was saying for a second and knew she had a valid point. She loved our brother just as much as I did, if not more, so I lowered the gun.

"Start talking," I said, just as the doorbell rang and then my phone right behind it.

"Who the fuck could that be?" Klimax asked. "I'll get it while you bitches sort this shit out. I swear y'all hoes be having the most drama ever. Need to start a muthafuckin' reality show," he said, walking off shaking his head.

"Hello." I answered the unknown number that had popped up on my phone. Usually I wouldn't dare answer an unknown number but today I welcomed the distraction. Too much shit was happening at one time.

"Girl, when the fuck did they start delivering mail on Sundays?" Klimax came back into the room holding a box addressed to me. I threw my finger up asking them to hold it down. Something in my soul told me shit wasn't right.

"Hi, my name is Michell Connelly with Baton Rouge homicide. May I speak with Cache Price?"

"Yeah, this is her. How may I help you?" I asked with concern written all over my face. My heart rate sped up not knowing what to expect from the other end of the phone call.

"Ma'am, we need you to come down to the homicide division. We have a few questions for you concerning your in-laws and we would rather not talk about it over the phone."

"What the fuck you mean? Where are my fuckin' children? Are they okay?" I asked. By now, my heart felt as if it had dropped into my ass. I could feel Tony staring me down when I mentioned the kids. As soon as he took a step closer to me, my instincts went back up and I stopped him dead in his tracks.

"Don't fuckin' move," I said, clenching my jaws as I held the phone to my chest.

"Are you still there?" I heard the detective say, once I placed the phone back to my ear.

"Yeah, I'm on my way. Say no more." I hung up without giving the detective time to respond.

"We gotta go," I said, tucking my gun in my back and grabbing my keys.

Tony

We finally made it to the Homicide Division and I still had no clue as to what the fuck was going on. But I knew one thing for certain, we were definitely about to find out. When Cache had answered her phone, I couldn't help but notice the look on her face. It was like she had seen a ghost, so I knew to expect the unexpected. I just hoped it had nothing to do with my kids, because I swear, I was gonna fuck Cache up on the spot.
"Hi, I'm Detective Connelly. Are you Cache Price?" she asked, with a polite smile spread across her face. She extended her hand and gave a firm shake.
"Yeah, that's me." Cache was worried and it was clearly written on her face.
"OK, well if you could step into my office we can get down to the reason I called you here. Could you all wait out here?" She asked, looking from me to Chanel, and then Klimax.
"No, if you don't mind it's okay for them to be in the room with me."
"OK, as you wish." Without further communication we walked behind fine ass Detective Connelly. One thing for sure was if we weren't being interrogated for murder or treated like criminals, according to the facts were the victims and not the suspects. "Have a seat," she offered kindly when we stepped into, what looked like, a conference room. That was when I felt a chill run up my spine, and something in my gut just didn't feel right. Everyone decided to take a seat but me. I just couldn't.
"I'm good," I said taking a stand instead.
"This is my partner, Homicide Detective Vincent.

"Listen, with all due respect could you tell us what the fuck we were called here for?" Chanel said. "Anytime you muthafuckas are being nice, someone died, no got killed, and you want a bitch to help with ya case. But if the shoe was on the other foot we would already be hogtied and gagged. So enough with the theatrics, please."

"Listen, every cop isn't like what you are stereotyping us to be right now ... but I'm gonna let that slide and move on to the more important things at hand. "I could tell ole girl had been born and bred in the hood by the slight neck roll she was giving Chanel while doing her best to keep it professional. You can definitely take the girl out of the hood but removing the hood out of the girl was a whole 'nother story.

"No, you listen bit—

"Chanel, please chill ... it's not the time nor place." Cache placed her hand on her sister's shoulder with pleading eyes. I knew it was because of the gun she had tucked in her back. That would definitely get her five years flat fa'sho. A convicted felon with a firearm? Wrong move. Chanel decided to sit back and chill after she'd read the expression on Cache's face.

"We're sorry to bring you this news but last night there was a break in at your in-laws' house and your father-in-law, Knowledge Duncan, was killed in the process.

"Where is Mrs. Duncan and my children! Please tell me they're okay?" Cache was the first to speak.

"Mrs. Duncan and Knasir are at the hospital—

It was my turn to cut her off now. "Where is my fuckin' daughter!" I shouted.

"That is what we haven't figured out yet. When we spoke to Mrs. Duncan she refused to talk to us and demanded that we retrieve her daughter-in-law so that's what we've done."

"Where is she now?" Cache spoke again as she stood up and grabbed her purse, ready to take off.

"Along with your son, she was taken down to Baton Rouge General to be medically assessed." Before Detective Connelly was finished talking the four of us were headed out the door.

At Baton Rouge General

"We're here for Knasir Price and Karen Duncan. They were brought in a few hours ago to be medically assessed," Cache spoke to the nurse at the intake desk.

"OK, let me type their names in to see what their room number is," she said. She quickly tapped the keypad of her laptop, typing their names into the computer. "They're both in room 201." With that information, we ran in the direction of the elevators.

Once we made it to the room, Cache was the first one to burst in the room.

"Ma, what's going on?" she asked Mrs. Duncan as soon as she stepped inside the room.

"Oh, baby!" Mrs. Duncan said, and as soon as she laid eyes on Cache's face, her sobs became uncontrollable. The scene in front of me was very heartbreaking, no lie. But I only had one question.

"Where is my daughter!" I tried keeping my voice at a medium especially considering the circumstances—her just losing her husband, the shit she had to witness, and us being in the hospital.

"Nigga, shut the fuck up!" If looks could kill I'd be dead.

"Look, bitch, this ain't the time or place for you to be acting like a fuckin' brat! I asked a legitimate question … the first muthafuckin' question *you* should have been asking. If you ask me, the shit is suspect like a muthafucka." I didn't give a fuck about the gun she had. I needed answers and expected to get them bitches even if it meant losing my life in the process.

"Suspect? Are you serious? No, what's suspect is how all of a fuckin' sudden you bond out, end up in my bed, and now my daughter done suddenly disappeared!"

"Hold up ... wait a minute, Cache," Mrs. Duncan stepped in between us.

"Momma, what's going on? Where is A'miracle?" Knasir woke up from all the commotion around him.

"It's okay, baby," she said, stepping toward him. Cache kissed him on his head and hugged him tightly.

"Chanel, take him to get something to eat, please. I know he gotta be hungry," Mrs. Duncan said.

*Knock. Knock.* We all turned toward the door.

"Is everything alright in here?" one of the hospital security guards opened the door to ask.

"Yeah, we good, homie." It was my time to speak. I had to let the nigga know I was the only man in the room and he wasn't welcomed. I didn't give a fuck who the nigga was.

"Alright, just keep it down. We have zero tolerance for disturbances. Have a blessed day." He bobbed his head and walked out with Chanel, Knasir, and Klimax right behind him.

As soon as the door was closed, Mrs. Duncan started telling us the events that had transpired from the previous night, all the way up to the point of us entering the room. After she was done telling the story, I wanted to kill Cache's ass more than I ever wanted to kill anyone before. "Who would have ever thought the bitch's promiscuous ways would fall upon our family?" I said out loud.

"*Promiscuous?* Nigga, kill that shit. Let's talk about where this shit really stems from. If you would've never sent that clown ass nigga to kill me I wouldn't have had to kill the nigga's brother! His bitch ass got exactly what he deserved! The nigga signed his own death certificate the moment he pulled the trigger and shot me but didn't shoot to kill," she screamed at me. The look on her face let me know she realized she'd said too much in front of Mrs. Duncan.

"You know what? I'm not about to continue to do this shit with you. Find my fuckin' daughter, bitch, 'cause if you don't, her husband won't be the only one she has to bury!" I said, walking out the door. I'd had enough. The sad part about all of it was I still loved the hoe. You would think that out of all she had put me through I would've washed my hands of her filth. *I need to focus*, I thought. *Right now is the time to love no one but myself, because at this particular moment, love don't love no one.*

There was a thin line between love and hate, and at the moment, I was definitely straddling the fence.

Maya

"SO HERE'S THE PLAN, MAMI," D'zyna said, and I was all ears. "I'm meeting that nigga Tony in less than an hour."

"Hold up, wait? I thought you said he wasn't fuckin' with you?" I was confused. "What happened?"

"Give me a minute to explain, hoe, damn. Honestly, I don't know what happened. Maybe the nigga had a change of heart, who knows. But what I do know is I plan on finding out where that bitch Cache is so you can stop all that fuckin' crying over the hoe. This situation is like spilling a glass of fuckin' milk. The only thing left to do is clean the shit up and keep pushing."

"Whatever, bitch. Just get me all the details and don't fuck it up."

"Girl bye. The only thing I got plans on fuckin' up is a bag, with no regrets."

"So what about the other plans we had for them bitches?"

"What? Setting that hoe Chanel's salon on fire? Consider it done, my love. I told you I got you. The niggas I hired said the only thing that would be left up after the flames are put out is the frames."

"Nah, I don't even want the foundation to be intact when the job is done."

"Got ya, cuzzo. Whatever you say. Your money, your way, love," she said, as she counted the money in the duffle bag I'd given her for the millionth time.

"Alright, that's the shit I like to hear. Get up with me when you get good news to show me I'm spending my money wisely and not wasting my time. You know the one thing I don't have patience for is wasting my time … or money. I gotta go back to Mexico to handle some business."

It had been a little minute since my mother Margaret died. The shit felt like I was grieving all over again. Just when I thought I could put the pieces of my life back together, things around me started crumbling like cookies. It had now been six months since Margaret's had been gone and my becoming a mother all at one time.

Here I was, a boss over my own empire, calling shots, and pulling triggers by word of mouth. Shit crazy. Having kids was never on my agenda but I can't say that I'm not use to it now. I must admit though, even still today it's a challenge. Just know I wouldn't give any of this up for the world, especially knowing the world is already mine. It doesn't matter that I didn't carry him for nine months. At first, my thoughts were to drop his cute butt off on Cache and Tony's doorstep but my heart wouldn't allow me to do so. No way would I have been able to do to my own flesh and blood what had been done to me. No, I didn't have the full story as to why my mother had thrown me to the wolves, but what I did know was normal people didn't just up and say fuck the child they'd birthed, no way. I was ready to lay my life down for the lil nigga just thinking about somebody harming him.

I looked down at him as he cooed, kicking his feet, and slobbering profoundly. I watched him, wondering where in the world did he fit. If there was any way possible I could stop him from going through all the heartache he was sure to endure from this cold world, I would.

"Momma loves you little guy, always remember that," I said, smiling down on him as I always did. "I don't give a fuck who or what tries to harm you, I'm going with my move straight-bangin' if so much as a hair is harmed on your little head, buddy. That's a promise, and you can bet your bottom dollar on that one lil man."

"Maria," I called out to help over the intercom.

"Sí, mami?"

"Come," I said, letting her know I needed her there and not where ever the fuck she was.

Within minutes, Maria was at my door knocking, instead of barging in. "You may enter," I said, as she jarred me from my current distraction.

"Yes?" Maria asked, in her thick Spanish accent as she walked through the door.

"Could you grab lil man for me, feed him, and place him in his crib for rest? It's past his bedtime."

"Sí. Would you like anything else, Ms. Maya?" she asked, as she grabbed Legend and his things.

"No, actually I'm about to head over and see my grandfather. Then after I'ma get a little rest myself. It was a long flight and it's weighing on me."

"Sí, mami, just call me whenever you need me," she said, smiling politely as she closed the door behind her.

Before leaving my room, I went to the wet bar and grabbed a drink. I settled for Cîroc. Without a second thought, I filled a shot glass, took it to the head, and followed it up with a second and third.

"Let me go see what's good with my grandfather," I said to myself. I could feel the effects of the alcohol kicking in quickly as I approached his room.

"Come in," came the deep voice of my grandfather as soon as I raised my hand to knock on his door.

"Damn, he's good," I said to myself as I entered into his personal space. "Where is everyone? Did you give everyone the day off or something?" I asked, as I spotted him sitting at his desk smoking a Cuban cigar.

"Actually, everyone is still here on guard. I decided to mix things up so I created a smoke screen instead. The third law according to *The 48 Laws of Power* is to: *Conceal your Intentions:* keep people off balance and in the dark by never revealing the purpose behind your actions. If they have no clue what you are up to they cannot prepare a defense. Guide them far enough down the wrong path, envelop them in enough smoke, and by the time they realize your intentions, it will be too late.'" My grandfather ended his words with that.

Knowing him the way I did and the many lessons he had taught me, I knew there were meaning and actions behind his words as always. So for the next couple of seconds, which felt like hours, we looked into each other's souls. I didn't want to be the one to break the ice so like a follower, I waited until my leader gave his command or simply dropped his jewels.

"I've been hearing things, and of course they haven't been good ... I try not to place myself in any of your affairs, but when they began to affect what I've built, then I'm being dragged into the middle of your fuckery!" Damn, shit traveled fast, but I wasn't that damn stupid to open my mouth, so I just listened. *Fuck, if he coming at me with it, ain't no sense in denying any of it,* I thought. "Remember, this is the life you chose. You wanna be the big Kahuna, so take my advice and start moving like one. Like the young folks say, get out your heart. There are too many bitches in this world to love or love you! Hell, you can even pay one to do whatever it is your heart desires, but his girl Cache is a troublemaker. Has been for a long while, plus someone close to her has been working with the FEDS for quite a while. If you still have plans to go along with your move, Law 29 says: '*Plan All the Way to the End*: The ending is everything. Plan all the way to it, taKing into account all the possible consequences, obstacles, and twists of fortune that might reverse your hard work and give the glory to others. By planning to the end you will not be overwhelmed by circumstances and you will know when to stop. Gently guide fortune and help determine the future by thinking far ahead.'"

By the time I left from my grandfather's quarters, my mind was in overload. Every word he'd spoken was the truth and like they say, the truth hurt. He was right about one thing fa'sho, I had enough money to make anybody do anything. I was definitely tripping, taking penitentiary chances, especially when I didn't have to. But of course, when the shit is personal there wasn't any amount of money in the world that would give you the same satisfaction of doing the deed yourself.

I just had to move smarter because I wasn't trying to lose the good future I had gained by default, fuck that! I needed to dead this shit with Cache immediately, before I allowed the bitch to take away more than I'd bargained for.

Tony

BITCHES CAME A DIME A DOZEN so why the fuck was I tripping over Cache? You would think it was clear that it was just time to give up whatever the fuck it was I was chasing. But if I had to be honest with myself, Cache had certainly become a drug to me. It felt as if I was chasing that first high, something all addicts (no matter the drug of choice) had experienced. That first high was a rush, and it was something you would never be able to obtain again in life. However, there was just something about her that wouldn't allow me to get her out of my system.

Like now, here I was lying beside a fine ass broad, whose back I had just finished blowing out. And when I say shawty let me take all of my aggression out on her, I fa'sho killed the pussy, but a nigga was still crying over spilled milk. Fuck it, I could admit my flaws.

I had been staying with D'zyna ever since I walked out on Cache, urging her to fix the shit between them. Truthfully, I just couldn't sit around without finding my baby girl, and without a doubt, the niggas responsible had to see me. Fuck the police and fuck whoever was coming behind the muthafuckas responsible for kidnapping my baby girl.

I decided to roll out of D'zyna's bed because one thing about it, I wasn't gonna find my daughter laid up with a bitch playing house.

"Honey, where are you going?" D'zyna asked, feeling the side of the bed I had been sleeping on.

"Out. I got a couple of things to do and I won't get any of it accomplished if I'm laid up with your fine ass all day." I chuckled, making light of the situation.

"OK, my baby. Give me a minute to freshen up so I can fix you some breakfast before you go," she said with a sexual coo in her tone. She would be sexy even if she tried not to be.

"Sorry, love, not today, but I'll make it up to you another time. How about that?" I declined her offer hoping I hadn't offended her in anyway. I had to admit though, she kind of fucked my head up because bitches these days were too emotional—always nagging and carrying on with the bullshit.

Something was up, but I just couldn't put my finger on it. I looked her in the eyes for a moment to see if I detected a snake. I couldn't, but that didn't mean shit. I knew a couple of bitches who held better poker faces than actual poker players. And on some real shit, at the moment, everyone was a suspect.

"Oh, okay ... well, just fuck with me when you can. I'll go shopping or some shit. Just make sure you come back through tonight. I want another shot of that dope dick you gave me last night."

After getting cleaned up and dressed, I headed across town. I needed to check niggas' temp, starting with the nigga Draco. The bitch nigga owed me money and hadn't made not one payment since my feet had touched the pavement on the free side of the fence.

Once I pulled up to the nigga's spot, the first thing I noticed was some niggas sitting out on the porch, but they were the least of my fuckin' worries. My baby girl was missing and I didn't give a fuck who I had to draw down on in order to find what was mine. I was in rare muthafuckin' form.

I hopped out of the car and moved with speed and precision. Instantaneously, the niggas posted up on the porch became alert, but weren't quick enough. Without further ado, I went for the pistol on my waist. Two niggas followed suit and made a motion to lift their guns as well, but it was useless. The big nigga on my left looked to be more so a problem than the one on my right.

*Pop! Pop!*

Two shots to the face did the nigga well and sent him on his way.

"Bitch, I wouldn't do that if I was you!" I shouted to the other guy. I watched the bitch-nigga shake like a hooker wearing a mini skirt on a corner in Chicago, determined to bring her pimp his money. "Where the fuck is Draco? Huh?" I asked. I closed the space between us and shoved my pistol in his mouth. "Open your muthafuckin' mouth!" I demanded, as I tried to stuff my gun down his throat. I jerked his gun from his hand, making him feel less than a man. "Give me your wallet." He did as I commanded. "Alright, 1617 Bluegrass—

"Look my nigga Draco ain't here, bruh." The nigga cut me off and started singing like a bird. "I swear on baby Jesus the nigga ain't here, but whatever I need to do to get you face to face with that nigga, I swear on my momma I got you. Bruh, just name it and you got it dawg, and that's on gang."

"Aight, get yo bitch ass in the house," I said, as I took the gun from his mouth and cracked him in his shit.

"Damn, bruh, why you do that?" the nigga had the fuckin' guts to ask.

"Nigga, shut the fuck up. If you try that pussy ass shit again, speaking out of the side of yo neck, I'ma blow your fuckin' brains out! You understand me, pussy?"

"Yeah, we good," he said. It was clear the muthafucka was shaking in his boots. If that wasn't a clear indication, the nigga had a trail of piss running down his leg. I shook my head at the nigga as I strolled behind him in the house.

"Give me ya fuckin' phone, bitch."

"Alright, mane. Are you gonna let me live after I set my nigga up?"

"Pussy, do you hear what you saying right now? Y'all niggas really kill me with that shit. You get in the game and when you get caught up in some street beef, you bitches always wanna ask a nigga to let you live. What part of the game is that? *Are you gonna let me live after I set my nigga up?*" I said mimicking the fool. "Sit the fuck down," I said, pushing him in a chair. I looked around the place to see what I could use to tie his ass up. *Bingo!* I thought. I walked towards an extension cord. I grabbed at least two of them and walked back toward that fool.

"Call that nigga Draco before I change my mind and splatter yo fuckin' brains all on this wall like paint on canvas," I said. I handed him the phone I'd taken from his pockets before hitting his bitch ass over the head again. This time the nigga started whimpering.

"Nigga, if you let on that something is wrong and alert that nigga, you might as well go 'head and say a prayer. You better ask the Lord for forgiveness and accept Him as your Lord and Savior," I said, lifting the gun to his head.

"Aight, I got it, bruh," he said, dialing the number.

"Put it on speaker," I demanded.

"Hello?" Draco picked up. "Nigga, this better be important. You know not to call me why I'm home chillin' with the fam.

"Yeah, my nigga, it's important. I need a re-up. The block hot and fiends comin' through like a nigga servin' hot cakes."

"Why the fuck you ain't call Dumbway?"

"Mane, the nigga ain't pickin' up. I went through my chain of command like you taught us and you the last hope."

## C.R.E.A.M. 3

"The fuck? Nobody pickin' up? What these niggas took off or some shit? Niggas like us don't celebrate holidays, birthdays, or none of that bullshit when it come to makin' money. Give me about ten. I'm 'bout to come through," he said. He sounded pissed but like the saying goes: ' a nigga would rather be pissed than pissed on'. In his case, I was definitely the one doing the pissing because I was about to wet that ass up. First, I had to get big boy's body and hide it behind the house.

Yolanda Moore

## CHAPTER 9
### CACHE

Sleep was hard to come by and I didn't know where the fuck to begin. I had been blowing Tony's muthafuckin' phone up and the nigga still hadn't answered the fuckin' phone. What kind of father did the nigga claim to be? I had been up for three days, too afraid I would miss something important. Now, I was damn near hallucinating. I was seeing shit, hearing shit, and I was fucked up. The current events hadn't made my situation any better.

"Cache, how are?" Chanel asked, as she stepped into the living room wrapped in a red silk robe.

"Fuck, no. I'm not. I been sitting here trying to figure out who the fuck would do some cruel shit like kill my father-in-law and take my fuckin' daughter?" I said. I rubbed my temple trying my hardest not to lose my fuckin' mind.

Something in my soul kept telling me to check Tony's ass. It was mighty funny the nigga ended up in bed next to me after all that shit happened, and now I couldn't remember any of the events of that night. "The only thing I remember is waking up next to that nigga," I said, running the moment I woke up to him, all the way to the minute the doorbell rang that morning. "Hold up!" I said, as I jumped up and ran to Chanel's room.

"Bitch, what?" she asked, running close behind.

"Where the fuck is that box Klimax came in here with? I just remembered when Tony and I was in the middle of arguing, I recall him bringing a box in the room addressed to me, right before we got that call from the detective." When I entered Chanel's room, my eyes landed on the box, and that's when I heard it. The sound of a phone ringing. I ran to the box and slid on the floor as if I was trying to make it to homebase before I was out. I ripped the box open as soon as my hands touched it. Inside was a ringing phone.

"Hello!" I shouted before I could even answer good.

"What took you so long to answer the phone? Is your daughter not that important to you?" I heard a robotic voice come from the other end of the phone.

"Yes, what kinda fuckin' sick-ass question is that?" I asked, breathing heavily through the phone.

"Listen, bitch, right game, wrong muthafucka. You are not in the position to be aggressive and shit. I know you would like to think this is your world and that Cache rules all, but newsflash, bitch. Your daughter's life is in my hands just like my brother's was in yours." That's when I remembered Mrs. Duncan saying some shit about CO's brother and then it hit me like a ton of bricks.

"Latray?" It was more a statement than a question. I knew his bitch ass looked familiar but I could never put my finger on the familiarity. Now I know why his bitch ass was so determined to get next to me and in my bed.

"What the fuck do you want from me?" I asked. But it was very obvious he was out for revenge. "I'll do whatever it takes ... just please don't hurt my baby."

"Bitch, was you thinking about not hurting my bro, hoe? Did you think about how his family would feel? His kids? Fuck no! So tell me why in the fuck I should grant the request you asking of me?" By this time, he had started talking in his normal voice and the robotic device he'd been using was gone. I had to come up with an answer that would appease him.

"Listen, Latray, you don't have to do this. My baby has nothing to do with my fuck-ups. Take me instead," I said. Tears began to flow down my face when I thought about the shit my baby had gotten caught up due to my fuck-ups.

"You know what? I must admit, I've grown to love both of your kids. But it's just you I got the fuckin' problem with, bitch. Since I'm feeling generous, I'ma let you work on getting your daughter back. How about that?"

"Just tell me what I need to do and I'ma do it."

"Alright, it's settled ... I need 5 million dollars within a week. Your first installment of 1 mill is due at the end of the week."

"I don't have that type of money. Where in the fuck do you expect me to get that type of cash from in a week?" I asked, already feeling defeated.

"You know what, fuck it," he said. Then I heard a gun being cocked in the background. "Kill the little bitch."

"No wait! I'ma get it. Just give me a little more time, please."

"Aight, you got that. And since that pussy is so good, I'ma give you some of this good dick. Anyway, I don't give a fuck how you gotta get me my money just get my shit! I don't care if you gotta rob a bank or rob every muthafucka in Baton Rouge to get me my 5 mill, just make sure I get me or I'ma send this lil bitch back to you in a wooden box!" Latray said, right before hanging up in my face.

"Bitch, where the fuck we gone get 5 million dollars from?" Chanel asked as soon as he was gone.

"I don't know. I'm trying to think," I said standing up, pacing the floor.

"How much money did you took from Tony? And what about the money Knowledge left you?"

"Good thinking. I know it's not gonna be five mill but at least it's a start. Where the fuck is Klimax?" I asked, realizing he hadn't been around since we'd left homicide. "He knows who to get in touch with in order to transfer the rest of the money out of that account. How much money do you have left from Carnel?"

"I still have all of it because we never decided what we were gonan do with it. As for the overseas account, I know who can transfer the money. Just give me a minute to get in touch with her," Chanel said, walking off to go handle her business.

I headed to my car to get the duffle bags of money I had taken from Tony. I had never gotten a chance to put the shit in a safe place. Good thing I didn't because there was no safer place than with me.

When I popped the trunk, I did a quick inventory and all the bags were accounted for. I decided to bring them all inside with me. My baby's life depended on me having that money and I wasn't willing to let a nigga j take it right from under my nose. They would have to kill me in order to get to it and it wouldn't be easy.

Finally, the last bag was thrown over my shoulder. As I headed back inside the house, a black Dodge Charger pulled up in front of it. My face instantly balled up as I reached for my hip. *Fuck!* Nothing was there. I must have left my shit inside. It would just be my luck to let a nigga catch me slipping. I turned to walk inside, never taking my eyes off the Dodge Charger. *Is it an undercover?* The passenger door opened.

"Girl, why the fuck you looking like that?" Klimax stepped out looking like he had just been fucked. Just before he closed the door I saw a white face. Or was I tripping?

"Bitch, you better be lucky I didn't have my heat on me because you and whoever that pink face muthafucka you rolling up with could have gotten the business just now and you don't even know it," I said, testing my theory.

"You damn right, I'm glad. But look, what's up? Have you heard anything?" he asked, quickly changing the subject.

# C.R.E.A.M. 3

I played right into his game though because I had bigger fish. *That muthafucka looked really familiar,* I thought, shaking the thought.

"Yeah, actually, I have. I'm glad you undecided to come yo ass home," I said, as we both stepped back into the house.

"So what's the plan?" Klimax asked, as I finished running the whole conversation down I'd had with Latray. "That nigga is ice cold. Who the fuck sleeps with a bitch, and the whole time plans a kidnapping of her baby, then on top of it all, ask for five mill? What the fuck you do to that nigga? I know he ain't doing all that just 'cause you robbed him," he said.

"Bitch, it ain't up for discussion, but I never said anything about robbery. Bitch, where you coming from with all these weird ass questions?" I asked, as my mind immediately fell back to the Dodge. Something in my gut told me something was wrong.

"Girl, you know Klimax is a weird ass individual, so don't even pay 'im no mind," My sister answered before he could. I swear if I didn't know any better I would think the both of they asses was fuckin' but I dismissed that thought as well.

"Alright first things first," I said as I began pulling money from each duffle bag. "We need to count this shit up 'cause in a couple of days, these niggas gonna expecting their first payment. Fuck! I wish I had a money machine to count this shit. I don't need them niggas playing games talkin' 'bout ain't I made the correct payment."

"Wait, sis … I think our brother had one stashed in the back somewhere. Give me a minute. I'll be back," she said. Chanel jumped off the couch and headed toward the back.

"Bitch, what's my task? I don't wanna be the one just sitting around looking all pretty and shit. I'm useful too, so use me," Klimax said, perking up. I thought for a moment, trying to think of what he could do.

107

"Give me a pen and paper. I need you to go to the store and grab me a few things," I said, as it dawned on me what I needed him to do.

"Bitch, I hope it ain't to go buy no groceries just 'cause you tryna get rid of me," he said, getting all in his feelings like he usually did.

"First of all, hoe … it's not going to buy groceries, and if you need validation on how important it is to go grab these items on this list, just know that your life depends on it," I said. I handed him the paper with a list of all the supplies I needed.

"Well since you say it like that, let me rise like yeast before I have to pay the piper." He took the list and headed out the door.

Ten minutes later, Chanel came back with the money machine. She kicked a laundry basket holding a block of money wrapped in Saran wrap. I touched my shoulders, then my forehead and chest, to signify the Cross, thanking my bro for looking out in desperate times.

"So, bitch, what's next?" Chanel asked.

"We gotta count this money up."

"I know for facts that all together it's over a million dollars. What are your plans? Do you think we should give him all of this at one time?" she asked.

"Fuck no! We definitely gonna play this nigga game exactly how he wants. Plus, I wanna be able to drop a bag every time the nigga come at my neck 'cause I know if I'm ever not able to pay 'im, or make one false move, ain't no telling how shit gonna turn out. I ain't willing to take chances with my baby's life like that," I said. The mere thought caused a cloud of tears to blur my vision, but I refused to let them fall. This wasn't the time to get all soft and shit. I needed to stay focused on what was important, and that was getting this bag to get my baby back.

"Alright, I get it," Chanel said. She busted the block of money so we could get the shit counted and bagged. "Sis—Chanel stopped midway to look me in my eyes.

"What's good?" I asked. She grabbed my hand.

"If we gotta stick a few muthafuckas up to get this paper, you can count me in. Matter of fact, I know just the right nigga to stick up and get all the money we need in order to get my niece back," Chanel said. Her facial expression displayed sadness.

"Who?' I ask curiously since my sister had never been down with my game; however, she had certainly piqued my interest.

"This guy name Mark. We been dating for like six months now, and I know he got the type of money we need." I thought about it for a second. The only Mark I knew that had that type of money was Mad Man Mark.

"Damn, sis, you really fuckin' with that nigga? That nigga got trust issues. He don't usually fuck with bitches like that. I heard the nigga only fuck hoes once, never twice 'cause he don't trust nobody." I looked at her with a questionable *are you sure?* look on my face.

"Bitch, yeah it's that nigga." She answered the question that was written on my face without me even having to ask it. "You not the only one who can pull a boss girl." She smiled.

"You sure you can do this?" I asked. I mean, she had been fuckin' with the nigga for six months and these days that was considered a lifetime.

"Yeah, bitch I can. I mean, I do love the nigga but you don't even have to ask who's more important. We already lost too many. A nigga comes a dime a dozen but family is forever. Bitch, you taught me that."

"Alright the shit settled then. You the captain of this ship, so tell a bitch what to do, and I'ma do it," I told Chanel, accepting her position of being in charge of our rules. I had always been the leader, but I knew when to take the back seat, and this was one of those times to do so.

Tony

AS PROMISED, IT ONLY HAD TAKEN Draco a few minutes to pull up on us. I looked at my hostage and placed my index finger to my lips, as a gesture for the nigga to keep his mouth shut. The lights in the living room had been turned off, so I peeked through blinds. I didn't need Draco to see my face.

"Do you remember what I said?" I asked dude.

"Yeah, bruh. When the nigga come in asking why the lights off, tell him I'm in the kitchen," he said. I could still hear his voice as it trembled a little but that was the least of my worries.

"Aight, don't let me down." I patted his shoulder as if I was encouraging him to do a good job, and in a way I was. I went and stood behind the kitchen door just as I heard Draco turning the knob on the door.

"Aye, Derrick!" Draco called out, "why the fuck the lights out, nigga?" he asked before flipping the light switch.

"My nigga, I'm in the kitchen," Derrick answered, just as planned.

"You still ain't answer my fuckin' question about these fuckin' lights! It ain't like y'all pay— What the fuck?" Draco blurted out, as soon as he entered the kitchen. I walked up behind him and snatched his gun off his waist as I pressed my chrome to the back of his head. "Derrick, you set me up, nigga? I'm ya fuckin' brother, nigga!"

"Bitch, don't nobody give a fuck about family no more, not even you, 'cause if you did, you wouldn't have a brother nickle-and-diming, nigga!

"Tony?" Draco asked, without turning around. My gun was still pressed to his head.

"The one and only, nigga. I know you didn't expect it to be nobody else. What? You thought a nigga was never gonna get out of jail?"

"Nah, bruh ... it ain't like that, but I got yo money if that's what this is about?"

"Now yo bitch ass wanna pay a nigga?" I said, shoving him to the chair before tying him with extension cords like I'd done his mans.

"Mane, are you gonna let me go now? I did exactly what you said, bruh," Derrick said just as I'd finished bounding Draco to the chair.

*Pow! Pow!*

"What the fuck, mane!" Draco yelled as his brother's blood splashed all over him. The pussy died with his eyes closed.

"Shut the fuck up! This my show you bitch ass nigga," I said then cracked him hard in his shit.

"Come on, mane ... I got yo fuckin' money, bruh. Plus, a ten percent interest on what I owe you," he pleaded.

"Oh, I definitely got plans on collecting my money 'cause there ain't a nigga walking God's green earth who ain't pay what's due to me. We gonna get back to that though. First, I need a few questions answered 'cause what I got going on is bigger than a bag," I said. I pulled up a chair and sat in it backwards. I crossed my forearm, one over the other. The hand holding the gun was on top.

"First off, I wanna say if it wasn't for niggas like you, niggas like me, a boss might I add, woulda been retired out the game. But you *bitches* just like hoes. Always looking for handouts. Now if I'm wrong, let me know I'm wrong. But something in my gut telling me you know who took my kid. And before you answer, I need you to think about what the fuck it is you gotta say." I tossed my head towards his brother Derrick and added, "Especially if you not trying to end up like that disloyal muthafucka you share the same blood with."

"Tony, I swear, nigga, I don't know shit about your daughter." Before I knew it, I shot his ass in the thigh.

"Aaahh, fuck mane! What the fuck yo do that for, bruh?" he asked.

"Because you know something and I swear I'ma get it out you," I said. I stood from my seat and looked for any kind of household product. *Bleach, perfect.* I walked over to the counter and retrieved it. "Whatever you fuckin' know, I'ma need you to spill it. Now!" I said, as I stood over him now with the bottle of Bleach.

"Mane, I'm telling- aaah- come on, dawg." I stuck my finger in the fresh bullet wound and poured bleach in it.

"Are you sure you don't know anything?" I asked. I wiped my face with the hand I'd just used to stick my finger in the hole in his leg.

"Latray, bruh ... I heard him and that nigga Nic owe Mad Man Mark some cash."

"Hold up, *Latray*, as in CO's brother Latray?" I asked, knowing the answer to the question.

"Yeah, bruh. Them niggas owe Mark money," he said. A whimper escaped his lips.

"Why the fuck they owe Mark?" The nigga was in the major leagues and he was me and CO's connect back in the day.

"All I know is I heard some shit about Mark, and he wasn't in the business for taking losses, so instead of CO's debt dying with him, it was handed down to his next of kin like a million-dollar insurance policy. That nigga Mark put a bag on CO's whole fam just in case them niggas ain't pay up. But you know that nigga Latray got a death wish on him, so the nigga ain't give a fuck at first. Then he heard his momma's name was also on the list. You just gonna let me bleed to death, bruh? Or are you gonna let a nigga go to the emergency room?" Draco asked.

"What the fuck Cache gotta do with this shit though. The shit seem too personal," I asked because, something just wasn't right but one thing I knew for sure is we needed to get to the bottom of this shit.

"The streets also saying Cache had something to do with killing CO. Nobody knows if she set the nigga up or if she was the one who pulled the trigger. That's the real reason Latray slid right up under her like the snake he is. Now on some life-and-death shit, my nigga, I'm not trying to bleed to death, so can you help a nigga out?" Draco looked up at me with pleading eyes.

"Sure," I said

"Thanks, my nigga."

*Pow!* I shot the nigga right between the eyes. I had never told the bitch ass nigga I had a daughter. All I said was my "kid" was missing. I never mentioned if it was a girl or boy. Even if the nigga didn't have direct involvement, he knew too much and didn't even send word to me. Everyone knew I fucked with Cache and they knew she was wifey. For a nigga to have that much info and not hit a nigga up meant we definitely had a problem with one another.

\*\*\*

AFTER LEAVING DRACO AND his brother slumped beside one another, I headed straight for Chanel's because I needed answers. I swear to God, whenever I caught up with them niggas, I was murkin' they asses on sight. One thing for certain, Latray had crossed a line that should've never been thought about crossing. At the end of the day, it was a dog-eat-dog world and if I didn't live by the rule before, a nigga definitely would now.

When I pulled up to Chanel's shit, I hopped out of my car without even parking it properly.

"Cache, where the fuck is my daughter," I yelled, and busted through the door with no regards. I was met with two guns pointed at my face. Cache stood behind one. Chanel behind the other.

"What the fuck you busting in my shit like that for, Tony? You almost got yo shit blowed back!" Chanel yelled. When she realized it was me she lowered her gun.

"Bitch, what the fuck you tucking your shit for? Fuck this nigga!" Cache yelled at Chanel yet her eyes or gun never diverted from me.

"Because, bitch! The nigga is not a threat to us and plus we got bigger fish to fry. Y'all can deal with whatever the fuck y'all got going on after we get my niece back," she said. She walked off leaving Cache and I to continue the stare-down which seemed like hours.

"You know what? Chanel is right. There's nothing more important than getting my fat momma back," Cache said. She lowered her gun to her side before turning her back on me. Then she walked off and took a seat on the loveseat, finishing counting the money that sat in front of them.

# C.R.E.A.M. 3

## Latray

"YEAH OLE BITCH ASS NIGGA, run me my money," I told Nic, as I held my hand out for the five hundred dollars I bet his ass on the football game. The Saints versus the Cowgirls. Our way 31-12. "Y'all bitches ain't fuckin' with us."

"Mane, fuck you. That shit was just luck," he said, giving me the money I'd won.

"I don't give a fuck what you call it. Luck or not, lil bitch, we won and I'm five hundo's richer," I said, stuffing my shit in my pocket without even counting it.

"Damn, nigga, turn the TV down. I think that fuckin' baby crying again. Bruh, we either gotta hurry up and get that money, give that crying ass baby back, or you need to call one of yo hoes to come and baby sit 'cause a nigga ain't got time for this bullshit."

"Nigga, who the fuck I'ma call? You know Jewel not fuckin' with a nigga."

"Bitch, if you knew how to get that hot ass temperature in check, maybe them bitches would be willing to stick around."

"Nigga, fuck all that, call yo fine ass cousin. I know she'll come through for a nigga. Make sure you let her gold-digging ass know I'ma break her off with some of this dick too."

"First off, nigga, none of my cousins wanna fuck with yo broke ass. Secondly, you gonna have to tell me which one 'cause all them hoes gold diggers, fine, and not to mention, you wanna fuck 'em all. And my nigga I gotta agree with you, 'cause if them bitches wasn't my cousins, I swear I woulda fucked all them hoes voluntary or involuntary," Nic said, grabbing his dick.

"Bitch, you really sound like a rapist, man. Nigga, I'ma start calling your ass Chester."

"Fuck what you talking 'bout. All them hoes grown. Now pass the weed, my nigga," he said, grabbing the blunt with the same hand he'd just groped his dick with.

"My nigga, you can kill that shit. I don't suck dick and ain't about to start," I said, before getting up to check on A'miracle.

"What's up, lil momma?" I said when I walked up to the bed. I picked her up to see if rocking her would help, but I knew why she was fussy. She missed her momma and she had a wet diaper. "Look, lil momma, I can accommodate you with one out of the two. Hold up, I'ma be right back," I said. I placed her back in the bed and she continued to cry as I headed out the door.

"Nigga, where the fuck you going? Don't leave me in here with that fuckin' baby crying, nigga." I could hear Nic continue to talk shit as I shut the door behind me.

*Knock. Knock. Knock.*

"Who the fuck beating on my fuckin' door this time of the fuckin' morning!" I heard my neighbor's old man call out.

"Nigga, answer the fuckin' door! This Tray," I said through the door.

"Look, young nigga, if you looking for Teedy she ain't here. I put that hoe out on the stroll." He began to close the door but I stopped it from closing by placing my foot against the door frame. "You niggas gonna start paying me for all the time you young niggas come looking for my bitch," he said, mumbling, just as my foot stopped the door and frame from connecting.

"Ain't none of them other bitches over here? Mane, I got my sister's baby over here and I need somebody to come change her."

"What you paying? 'Cause any bitch who sleeps under this roof sells pussy, mouth, and ass, but I can do the shit myself if you paying my nigga," he said, scratching his arm. I knew the nigga was thinking about a hit, and probably his first of the day.

For a moment, I looked the nigga up and down and considered letting him change the baby.

"Nah, I'm good." I turned around to head back to the house.

"Nigga suit yaself. I might not look like it but I used to run and own a daycare, except all the bitches were grown," he said and closed the door behind him.

"What the fuck took you so long, nigga?" Nic asked as soon as I opened the door. "Why the fuck you ain't come back with somebody?"

"Nigga, stop asking all them fuckin' questions before I start thinking you working with them people. And did you call ya cousin D'zyna yet?"

"Nah, my nigga. You was serious? I thought we wasn't putting too many people in our business, dawg? I'm telling you now, I'm not going to jail for kidnapping no baby. I might go to jail for pushing a nigga melon back, but a baby? Fuck that! I'ma call that bitch 'cause I'm not changing no diapers, but I'm telling you now, cousin or no cousin, that bitch open her mouth, I'm closing her curtains."

"Nigga stop all that pussy ass crying and call yo fine ass cousin."

\*\*\*

"I KNOW ONE MUTHAFUCKIN' thing, you niggas better run me them five big faces," D'zyna said stepping through the door. The bitch made me want to fuck her sexy ass right where she stood.

"Come yo thick ass here and sit on a nigga's lap," I said, patting my leg.

"Nigga please run me my muthafuckin' money before we have problems in this bitch. Big facts."

"Damn it, I love when you talk that gangsta shit," I said. I dug in my pocket to get her the money. "Nigga, I should make yo bitch ass come up outta pocket. I ain't say shit about five hundred but I see you game. The nigga really mad 'cause I bet his sorry ass football team and we stomped that ass," I said laughing.

"Nigga same thang that'll make ya laugh will make ya cry. Now run my cousin her shit."

Oh trust, I'ma pop it off, but trust me when I say I'll definitely be compensated later for the difference." I smiled up at her as she snatched the money from my hand.

"Now what is it that you niggas need me to do?" she asked, standing in front of me with her weight mostly on the left side, and her right hand on her hip.

"My sister's baby is here and I need help with her."

"A baby? Who in the fuck would leave their child with you niggas? And Tray I didn't know you had a sister. I thought it was just you and CO?"

"See, and that's exactly why you need to give a nigga a chance so we can get to know each other on a more personal level, sweetheart." I smiled and grabbed her hand off of her hip.

"Damn, D, you asking too many questions. Just do what the fuck we paid you to do," Nic said butting in.

"No nigga, I'm not asking enough questions. For all I know, you niggas probably got me caring for one of y'all's hoes kids," D'zyna said, never taking her eyes off me. "No telling when it comes to y'all asses. So fuck my question?

Nah, nigga, fuck you. Now let me go see what I'm dealing with." She strutted her fine ass to the back.

*Knock. Knock. Knock.*

"Damn, nigga, you expecting somebosy?" Nic asked as he grabbed his and walked toward the door. "Who the fuck is it?" he asked, peeking out of the peephole. Oh, it's Teedy. Bitch what the fuck you want?" he asked again, as he opened the door.

"*Bitch*? Nigga you muthafuckas was looking for me. I'm the *bitch* who should be asking what the fuck you niggas looking for me for? I know it ain't to get none of this good pussy, is it?" she said, rubbing Nic's chest

"Bitch, get yo crusty cum fingers off me before five of them nasty muthafuckas come up missing," he said. He pushed her hand off of him causing her to stumble. I couldn't do shit but laugh at them because every time they came in contact with each other, that was the kind of shit that happened between them.

"If y'all don't stop acting like this every time y'all in each other's company, I'ma start thinking you paying Teedy to fuck."

"Nah, baby, he ain't gotta pay to fuck me," she said, licking her crusty ass lips. Nic closed the door in her face and left her standing on the other side.

"Fuck both of you niggas. I'ma take my good pussy and money somewhere else where I'm 'preciated," she shouted through the door. She kicked it and then stormed off.

"Aye, what's her name? And do you niggas have pampers? Food? A bottle?" D'zyna asked, stepping out of the room to grab my attention.

"Her name is A, um… A- A'miree, yeah, that's it. But look, can you grab all that other shit you just named? And promise not to label a nigga unfit?" I said. I reached back in my pocket and grabbed a knot of money.

"Thanks, and I'll think about it." She grabbed my money from my hand and bent down and kissed me on my cheek. Just as I turned my neck to kiss her on the mouth, she took her manicured hand to my face and pushed it back.

"Give me a couple hours with her and I'ma get lil momma back quiet. She gonna be full, dry and clean."

"D, where the fuck you taking her?" Nic asked. He jumped up and blocked his cousin from leaving.

"Nigga, what the fuck you mean? I'm doing what y'all paid me to do. Now get yo retarded ass out my face and path before I change my mind. Nigga you 'bout to make me have a sick mind, and my next question since I got so many, 'bout to be did you kidnap this poor baby?"

"What?" Nic and I blurted out at the same time. "Fuck no!" we both said again.

"Nic, let her do what she came over here to do, nigga." He stepped aside and let her walk out the door.

"Dawg, you trippin'," I said, as soon as D'zyna was out of earshot.

"Nah, I ain't trippin' hard enough! And nigga you too laxed for me. You act like you been doing shit like this all yo life," he said, rolling another blunt.

"Nigga, real shit? You better be lucky you my nigga 'cause I woulda been filled that ass up with lead," I said. I shook my head as my mind quickly switched gears thinking about the five-million-dollar payday.

C.R.E.A.M. 3

# CHAPTER 10
## CHANEL

As I stood outside of Mark's mansion, I took a minute to gather myself before I placed my thumb on the fingerprint scan to unlock the front door. "Babe?" Where are you? I'm home," I said, walking to the kitchen to put the groceries up.

"Hey, love," I heard Mark say behind me, as he wrapped his arms around my midsection.

"Oh my God. You scared me!" I said, jumping at the same time. I dropped the pancake mix I was placing inside the pantry.

"Sorry, baby," he said. He kissed me on my neck."

I turned in his arms to face him. "Where yo fine ass been all my life?" he asked, kissing me in my mouth. Damn, the nigga was so handsome and sweet. It was so hard to picture him as the monster the streets made him out to be.

"I been right here, baby. You just couldn't find me but I'm glad you finally did." I smiled and kissed him back.

"Me too. Listen, leave that shit right there or let the help get the shit. I don't pay them just to chill at my crib.

"I know, baby, but you know I love making sure my part is taken care of. I don't need you having other bitches doing what I can do," I told him as my jealousy showed.

"Baby, that's something you will never have to worry about. There ain't a bitch alive who could ever fill your shoes. You understand me?" Mark asked, grabbing my chin

"Yeah I understand, daddy," I said shyly. Damn, I loved that man.

"You know what? I think you should go freshen up and put one of your shopping outfits on so we can go fuck some money up." He kissed me again.

"Honestly, I was thinking since you spoil me so much, I would like to repay you the favor so how about we both go freshen up. I'ma go cook us something to eat and then serve you *me* on a platter as your dessert. What do you say?"

"I say fuck shopping, and let's go with your plans. I like them better than spending my money on you." He laughed as I pushed him off me

"Negro, please," I said, walking off, as he slapped my ass making it jiggle. I put an extra twist in my step that said I was a confident woman with a whole lotta attitude. I had to remind him why he chose me in the first place.

"Chanel, don't make me fuck you up!" he yelled, playfully running behind me.

"Oh, you can fuck me up. Just make sure you good at it, my baby," I said and took off running from him. I hadn't even made it across the kitchen doorway before Mark caught me. I fell straight to the floor and balled up because I knew exactly what was to come.

"Don't resist this shit, baby girl. There's no way you can talk your way out of this.

"Not even if I give you the best head you've ever had? Please, don't tickle me. I'll do whatever it is that needs to be done ... pleaseeee, I'm tapping out, baby," I said, as he went for the gusto. Ha, ha, ha, ha, ha, pleasssee!" I continued to laugh hysterically.

*Ding Dong!* The doorbell rang and grabbed our attention.

"Yes! Saved by the bell," I said, as soon as he got up off of me.

"You lucky, girl," he said. He reached for my hand and helped me up off the floor.

"No, you lucky, because I was just about to fuck your ass up, Mark." I laughed and walked off to go handle my wifely duties. As I was headed up the stairs to freshen up, I looked back toward the front door and noticed a dude walking inside. *Fuckin' hoodlum. I can clearly see he's not on Mark's level*, I thought, immediately checking out attire.

"What's good, boss man," I heard our visitor say

"I'm hoping you can tell me what's good, Nic. I'm becoming impatient waiting on you niggas to come through with my money."

"Dawg, I swear on baby Jesus, we working on getting you yo shit. Matter of fact, we gone have your hands greased by tomorrow, and that's on my life."

"You fuckin' right it's on yo life, because that's exactly what I'm taking if the two of you nigga don't come through with my shit," I heard Mark say before his voice faded. One thing I didn't do too often was stick my nose into Mark's affairs.

As soon as I made it to the bedroom we shared whenever I did decide to stay over, I began to feel nauseated.

"Oh fuck!" I said running to the bathroom. "Awwee." I made it just in time. I managed to throw up in the toilet instead of on the floor. "Something ain't right," I said aloud to myself. That's when I thought about the pregnancy test Klimax had bought me before all the shit popped off with Cache. When Klimax first gave it to me, of course it had been a joke. But now that I thought about it, I wasn't too sure if it was after all.

After taking a few minutes to gather myself, I went downstairs to my car to grab the pregnancy test out of my purse. I ran back up the stairs trying my best to avoid Mark. Something deep inside of me told me I was with child. But knowing what I knew, it was kind of hard for me to face him. *But I had to do it in order to bring A'miracle home*, I thought placing my hand on my stomach. Without a doubt, I know Cache would come through for me if the shoe was on the other foot.

Once I made it back to the room, I went straight to the bathroom and closed the door. I placed my back against the door.

"Come on, girl, you can do this," I whispered as I coached myself to go through with taking the test. But did it really matter if I knew my truth? If I was pregnant I wasn't even sure if I would keep the baby. My baby.

I came out of every piece of clothing I had on and watched them fall into a heap on the floor. I started running my bath water.

"Fuck it," I said, stepping from the tub to grab the test. I opened it quickly and peed on it before I lost the courage to go through with it. Once it was done, I proceeded to the tub to handle my womanly duties.

***

"CHANEL! ARE YOU FUCKIN' KIDDING ME!" I heard Mark shouting over me.

"What?" I jumped out of a deep steep. "Babe, you scared me. What are you so excited for?" I asked.

"What am I excited for? Love, you just made me the happiest man alive is what." That's when it hit me. I was pregnant! I had to be. What other reason would he be that excited. Fuck, I fell asleep before I even had a chance to hide the test. I never even had a chance to look at it myself.

"I can't be," I said to myself as I looked at my pruned fingers.

"Hold up, wait. What? You don't want to be? You're not just as excited as I am?" he asked, with his face screwed up.

"No baby, I am. I'm just shocked is all," is what my mouth said, but my mind screamed *why me Lord!*

# C.R.E.A.M. 3

Here it was: I had always wanted children and a family. And Mark was the perfect man to have that with. There wasn't too many niggas from my neck of the woods who were that excited and devoted to want to be a father, and here it is I was about to fuck it all up.

"Mark, I can't have this baby," I said quickly, not meaning the words to come out.

"What? What the fuck you just say?" he asked twice, as if he hadn't understood what I'd said.

"What the fuck do you mean?" He asked another question before I could even respond to the first two.

"Baby, I'm scared. What if I have to do this all on my own?" I asked, placing blame on him as if he was the reason for my decision.

"Oh no, baby, come here," he said, softening his aggression because of my different approach. But what I was thinking about was how he would hate me once he figured out I had been the one who set him up.

As he helped me out of the tub, I couldn't help but cry. I cried for myself because I had already deemed myself a single mother and I cried for my child because he/she wouldn't have a stable two-parent home. I had always wished and hoped for my children to have a more stable home than me and my sisters and brother had ever thought of having.

I continued to cry as Mark took his time drying then lotioning my body ever so gently. All I could think about was us living in our last days of enjoying one another. My mind shifted to asking him for the rest of the ransom we needed, but no way would he be willing to come up off of that much money just for me and my family.

Not realizing Mark had completely dressed and tucked me in the bed, he had taken his spot beside me and held me in his arms. He gently kissed the top of my head and rocked me until everything surrounding me went black.

***

The next morning when I awoke, I knew I needed to get my emotions in check. I needed to get my niece back and whatever came behind it then so be it. I got my emotional ass out of the bed to fix my nigga breakfast. It would be a horrible time for me to start losing trust that I had worked so hard to gain. A bitch worked hard to break through to him and now all of my hard work would certainly pay off.

I wasn't sure of Mark's whereabouts but if I had to bet my Burke, he was in his study ducked off handling business. I didn't mind though because I needed the little extra time to recuperate. I took my time prepping breakfast for the king, and when I was done, I was ready to serve him French toast, scrambled eggs, Jimmy Dean sausage links, and a tall glass of freshly squeezed Florida orange juice. I wasn't sure if the shit was actually from Florida but it sounded good.

Once his breakfast was neatly placed on the serving tray, I straightened my back and walked into the study with a big smile on my voice.

"Good morning, baby. How did you sleep last night?" I asked, as if I was avoiding my episode from last night.

"I didn't sleep too well worried about you, but it's not about me right now. The question should be how do you feel? Are you okay?" he asked, concerned.

"Actually, I am. I know I was a little emotional last night."

"*A little?*" he asked. Now he was smiling up at me as I took a seat on his lap.

"I know, baby. I shouldn't have overreacted but I honestly didn't know if you would be around to help me raise her?" I said holding my stomach.

"*Her?*" Nah, that's my lil nigga in the oven," he said, placing his hand over mine. "But look, love"— he grabbed my chin and looked me in the eyes as he spoke—"I don't know what kind of lames you used to, but I ain't the one. I'm cut from a different cloth, and niggas like me, which there ain't many of me roaming the earth, don't do no pussy ass shit by not taking care of their responsibilities. I'ma real one, lil momma, so don't ever put me in the category with them lames. You understand me?" he asked. He pecked me on my lips.

"Yeah, and I'm sorry for doubting you, and you right, I'll never do it again. Now enjoy your breakfast, baby. Let me go clean the kitchen."

\*\*\*

"SIS, YOU HOME?" I shouted, as I walked inside my living room and placed my keys on the end table.

"Yeah, bitch I'm in here. Where the fuck you been for the last week?" Cache asked from the kitchen.

"By Mark's house." I answered and she stopped doing what she'd been doing to look at me.

"So what's up?" she asked

"All work no play, huh?"

"You know I quit school because of recess," she said seriously.

"Well, I been planning how we gonna do this shit, and I think I've come up with the perfect plan."

"OK, I'm listening."

"Could yo impatient ass let me talk and stop interrupting me, bitch, damn! So, as I was saying, Mark asked me to go out of town with him and of course I said yes. I might as well go and have a good time before the nigga drop me on my head or even worst, kills me. Well, he might not kill me because I'm pregnant ..." Damn, my fuckin' mouth!

"*Pregnant!* What do you mean? As in you having that nigga's baby? Fuck!" She slapped her forehead and started pacing the floor. "No way are you gonna be able to do the shit now because you're too attached."

"I got this, and if you seriously think my niece means less to me and Mark means more, then you don't know me like you claim!" I said yelling now.

*Ring. Ring.*

Before Cache had the opportunity to get in my ass like I knew she truly wanted to, "the phone" rang and I figured it must have been time to make the first ransom drop.

Nic

"MANE, TRAY YOU MY BRO and you know I'm with whatever when it comes to you, but son you really got a nigga holding a baby hostage, feeding 'em chicken nuggets and shit. Then to top it all off. it's a lil girl, bro. All I kept thinking about is if a pussy lay a finger on Jamya or Malassia, Lord knows I'ma be doing every bit of life and a dark day, because I'ma bury the whole fam behind mine," I said, knowing my nigga was gonna really feel some type of way. But I had to get the shit off my chest because I wasn't trying to go to hell for the shit. "Nigga what happened to no women or kids? We coulda at least snatched that grimy-ass hoe of yours. I know her nigga would break his neck to up five mill for the bitch."

"Nic, what the fuck pussy? You need to lay off that fuckin' liquor before that shit get you fucked up. And when the fuck have you gain a conscious? And to be honest, you ain't never gave a fuck about nobody but yourself! So spare me the bullshit you spittin' 'bout women or children. Besides, don't act like a nigga ain't been planning this shit for months now. You just refused to see the shit! The time is here and now, and now you wanna get cold feet on a nigga? You acting like a hoe and the shit got me feeling like this shit might turn out bad in the end 'cause of you. Maybe I should handle you right now!" Tray screamed back at me as spit flew out of his mouth.

"Nigga we talking five million fuckin' dollars ... an easy five million that you ain't got to do shit for but "babysit". I don't know a nigga that wouldn't love to be in your shoes. Nigga, I'm the one who been faking to like the bitch knowing the hoe killed my brother. I woulda been smoked her ass if it wasn't for the bounty that nigga Mark put on my whole fuckin' family's head because of my brother's fuck up! Bruh, this shit is too sweet. We only owe that nigga two mill and the rest will definitely put us back in the game, baby—a place we ain't been since my brother died. So who gives a fuck what it takes? Fuck love *and* having a heart!"

"You right, my nigga," I said, agreeing. But no lie, the shit made plenty of sense now.

"I know I'm fuckin' right. You think that hoe thought twice about taking CO from my momma? Fuck no! So it's fuck her and this lil bitch. She'll be lucky if I don't smoke both of them once we get that bag."

Even though I agreed with some of the shit he said, I didn't agree with it all. I still wasn't down with killing no kids. Fuck what he talking about, and on everything I love, if he attempted to do the unforgivable, I was definitely gonna be the person standing behind the smoking gun that killed him.

"Look, son, you already know I know what's up. I went through it all with you from day one, so I'll never fold. You right though, we need this money to get Mark off our backs because the nigga ain't gonna hold out too much longer, and I'm tired of prolonging this shit too. I'm ready for it to all be over just as much as you, Tray. I'm tired of watching over my shoulders every time I take a step, anticipating whether it's my time to go to jail or hell.

At the end of the day, I know in the end that's the only two places I'm destined to end up. Just know you my nigga, and you never alone. Matter fact, " I said, picking up my throwaway, "it's time for the broad to stop with the games and drop that first bag." I hit Facetime and placed the screen in front of A'miracle until Cache's voice was heard over the loudspeaker of the iPhone.

"Oh my God, my baby! Please, don't harm her," I could hear her crying.

"Bitch, I'm hoping you about to bring music to my ears. What you got for me?" I asked, cutting straight to the chase as I focused the phone on my ski-masked face.

"I got what you asked me for—one million in cash." Damn Tray was right. That bitch didn't play. I had to give it to her, the bitch moved better than most niggas out there.

"Bet, meet me at 5504 Arbor Vitae Dr. The green abandoned house at 10 p.m. And bitch, I know how you scandalous bitches get down, so don't play no games because A'miracle will need a miracle if you do."

C.R.E.A.M. 3

# CHAPTER 11
## LATRAY

Something was up with my dude, yo! Yeah, I knew this type of shit was new to him but I wasn't used to the nigga having a conscience. All this shit coming from a nigga who had more bodies under his belt than water in the ocean. I was really despising the nigga's vibe and I just asked the Lord not to let the nigga betray me.

"Nic, I'm 'bout to step out and make a call to Mark for a linkup since you handled the other lil business. A mill gotta give us some lead way with the nigga. Fuck, that's half of what we owe dude in one wop. As for the rest, she'll have that shit in no time then a nigga can move around free."

"Yeah, a'ight. And hurry up 'cause it's yo turn to feed this lil greedy muthafucka. Aye," he called right before I could hit the door. "What happened to you calling some hoes over here? Nigga tired of bussin' yo ass in 2K. I wanna bust something else up, something nice too."

"Whatever, nigga," I said and walked outside the door, dialing Mark's number. "Yo, Mark, my nigga, what's good?" I asked as soon as he picked up.

"This nice view of ya momma's crib, but not for too long if I don't get my fuckin' money, nigga."

"Yo, whoa, hold up! I know you not with the shits in front of my mom's crib dawg. What the fuck, bro? I swear to God. Look, mane, we got a mill for you right now, ready to link up. So chill son!"

"Say less. Now you talking my language, nigga. Come fuck with me. Meet me at 12:00 a.m. at the Let Out. (the Let Out was a place where people were known to conduct business," he said, before the phone disconnected.

"Fuck!" I screamed, shaking my head. *Bitch-made nigga playing too close to home,* I thought and called my mother.

"Hello, Ma? What you doing?" I asked, before she could even fully accept the call.

"Nothing, my baby, just sitting outside enjoying this nice weather. Probably about to water my garden before I go inside."

"Oh, okay. Well hurry up, and be safe. Love you."

"Love you too, Latray, but why you rushing me off the phone? Where are you? You know how I worry about you ever since that happened to your brother, you know?"

"I'm on the other side of town but don't stress yourself about me. You know I'ma come through and see my old bird later on," I said smiling.

"OK, well, be safe, my baby. I'ma cook something for you because I know you haven't had a home cooked meal in forever." I laughed because she was so right.

"You right, Ma. I can't wait. I'll be there soon, Ma. Love you," I said, trying to get her off the phone because I know if I didn't she was going to start.

"Love you too, boy, and see you soon." We hung up, promising to see each other later.

"Yo, what's up, pussy boy? Everything together?" Nic said as he came outside. "And nigga why yo facial expression giving me troubled? What's poppin'? I'm guessing this fool just ruffled your feathers, huh?" Nic asked.

"Man, fuck dude. Let's just get this money so we can meet tonight. And let that hoe know I want the rest by Friday afternoon! No fuckin' exceptions!" I said.

"Bet, I'm ten toes down, bruh. But one question ... Who's babysitting tonight? Do I need to hit up one of my ratchets or you already got that covered? Whoever the bitch is I gotta make sure them bitches stop and pick up a few groceries, some

## C.R.E.A.M. 3

Hot Pockets and shit. Damn, nigga, don't let me forget some drank and 'Gars, and diapers. Fuck, I'm the nigga that feel like I'ma hostage. I ain't been nowhere or seen nobody in days," he said, shaking his head.

"Nigga, stop all that fuckin whining like a lil hoe, Nic. The more I think about it, the more I'm thinking I shoulda left yo ass broke and on ya ass. I never knew you was so delicate. You acting like you get a period every month," I said, shaking my head, blowing it!

"Get the fuck out of here and make the call. I'ma go prepare myself for tonight."

Yeah, that nigga got a period. *What nigga gotta prepare they self?* I thought, and laughed.

### D'zyna

"HELLOOO," I SAID GETTING AGGRAVATED. I just knew Latray didn't have one of his little scandalous bitches playing on my line and the nigga wanna call me scandalous.

"Damn, D'zyna, why you hollerin' in a nigga ear? I don't wear hearing aids, sexy." He laughed.

"Boy, I kept saying hello and you didn't answer for a lil minute. I thought one of your bitches was playing on my phone and I was definitely ready to pull up on that ass and show them hoes. You and her. I'm not the bitch to play with," I said seriously.

"Damn, lil momma, you ready to fight behind a nigga, huh?"

"Please. You wish. There's only two things a hoe like me get down and dirty for and a dick ain't one of them."

"That's cold, lil momma," he said, as if his feelings were truly hurt.

"Don't shoot me because I don't get down like a regular, love, but it's the truth."

"Aight, that's cool, but tell a nigga what makes you break a nail?"

"If a bitch or a nigga fuck with my bag and my weed, it's up." I laughed just fuckin' with him. "And in that order."

"You serious?"

"Sure am. But look, what's up? 'Cause I know you didn't call to fuck with me or talk on the phone like we back in high school."

"Actually, you correct, but why you tryna rush a nigga off the phone? You got another nigga over there sniffing what's mine?"

"Boy, no, but don't get it twisted, I can," I said. I was still fuckin' with him but truthfully, Tony was on the way over to my crib to blow my back out just the way I liked it. I kept that as a thought though.

"Don't I know it. But nah, I'm calling 'cause I need you to watch my sister's baby again."

"Not gonna happen, homeboy."

"Come on baby, please?"

"If I didn't have plans I would, especially since A'miree is such a pleasant baby to be around. As far as her being your sister's baby ..." she said and paused, "I'm starting not to believe that shit but I'ma let the shit slide. I'm sorry though 'cause I'm busy for the night. Listen though, I'm in the tub, so give me a call tomorrow. If you still need me to come through then I got you."

"Aight, bruh," he said, and hung up before I could say anything else.

"Ole, well... fuck it. He must've been in a rush," I said, finishing up in the bath before Tony popped his sexy ass up.

# C.R.E.A.M. 3

\*\*\*

After rubbing myself down in lotion, I put on a sexy lingerie number from Victoria Secret. I was ready to be fucked out of it, and I wanted the lotion to mix with the sweet hot smell of sex.

"Damn, how did I forget to put this back on A'miree before I took her back to Tray?" I said to myself. When I heard the doorbell ring, I placed the gold bracelet back on the nightstand. "I'm coming, bae," I yelled, prancing my ass to the door in a pair of six-inch heels. *Nigga better fuck my ass to death tonight or we definitely gonna have some problems in this bitch tonight*, I thought. I smiled as I opened the door wide to give him a view of what he had left high and dry for the past week or so.

"What's good, love?" he asked. Once he'd stepped inside, I stepped aside and gave him enough space to walk past me.

"Nothing, daddy. Been waiting on you to come through is all," I said, as I closed the door. My hot pussy ass didn't waste any time. I pounced on Tony with no remorse whatsoever. Maya was right, 'if I wasn't careful, the nigga would be easy to fall for'. The little time we'd spent together had already gotten me attached, not to mention, he fucked me righteously. He was just as delicate as he was when he applied pressure, giving me nothing but pleasure and pain.

"Hold up, D, let's take this to the room," he said, stopping me as I took it upon myself to relieve him of his clothes. *Fuck what he talking about,* I thought, *life too short for procrastination.* So, instead, we continued ripping each other's clothes off, and left a trail of his clothing from the living room to the bedroom.

The center of my lingerie was missing for easy access. Like I said, no time to wait. I lay across the bed on my back and spread my legs like butter on bread, all the while, playing with my clit.

"What the fuck you waiting for?" I asked Tony as he stood over me gazing. "We've both waited long enough. Come fuck me ... now," I demanded. He placed his gun on the nightstand and crawled his necked body into my bed. He touched my body with his chilled hands and his touch made me moan, "Tony, yeeeess!" I said, as he pushed my breasts together and used his thick tongue to flick at my nipples at the same damn time.

I could feel his dick growing harder between my thighs. Knowing what was to come made my pussy juices flow down my ass. I grabbed his rock-hard dick and placed the tip at the opening of my split wetting it with my hotness.

Once he felt my middle, I knew it would be hard for him to resist. In one swift motion, he thrust inside of me with no regard. Simultaneously, he wrapped one hand strongly around my neck just the way I liked him to.

Tony

Damn, D'zyna's pussy was so wet and tight, I could literally drown and get stuck in it. I was trying my hardest not to cum but it was becoming hard to hold back. She began working her hips to my rhythm and I knew my time was near. Her moans grew louder the more I picked up the pace. My grip on her neck grew stronger making her pussy wetter, and her walls gripped me like a vice.

"I'm cummin', Tony, fuck!" She pushed the words out as my hand made them hard to escape her mouth and penetrate the air. She dug her nails into the skin on my back and bit down on her bottom lip. The shit drove a nigga crazy. No lie, at first I wasn't with the choking shit until she talked me into it and squirted on my dick. I guess that first time was *my* first time to learn why you shouldn't say what you'll never do, because I been choking her ass ever sense.

"Cum for me," I moaned in her ear. My eyes rolled in the back of my head and my toes began to curl as I came inside her.

That's when I noticed *it* sitting by my gun on the nightstand. A'miracle's bracelet sparkled. I knew it was hers because I'd had it custom made and it had been the only one ever made. I looked from the bracelet to D'zyna as she continued to cum. I couldn't help myself as my grip grew stronger, and it was like I started having an outer body experience. She started clawing at my hands and pushing my face while trying to say something but I couldn't understand her. I had blacked out.

"Bitch, where the fuck is my daughter? Huh? You in with the niggas who kidnapped her?" I said, asking question after question. "Talk bitch!" I screamed. I felt like I was losing my mind. That's when I realized that even if she wanted to say something, she couldn't because she had just taken her last breath.

"Fuck!" I jumped up realizing I had been sleeping with the enemy the whole time. *How the fuck did this happen?* I mentally asked myself as I paced the floor trying to figure out my next move. *Damn!* She was so close but yet so far away. I quickly dressed with no time to waste.

I started searching around her bedroom looking for something—a clue that would lead me to finding my baby girl. Then as I continued to search, I realized my only connection to my daughter was her bracelet. I picked up her bracelet and held it in my hands as tears welled my eyes. *I need to get out of here and find my fuckin' daughter!* I thought as I kissed the bracelet and slipped it inside my pocket. Next, I grabbed my gun and headed for the door.

# Yolanda Moore

*Ring. Ring. Ring.*

I heard D'zyna's phone ring as soon as my hand touched the door knob. I looked back at the living room table where it was. I walked over where it sat, picked it up, and looked at the screen.

The name "*Maya*," popped up. *Whoever that is won't be hearing from D'zyna until they meet her in Heaven or Hell,* I thought. I grabbed her phone and slipped that in my pocket as well and then got the fuck outta dodge, because just that quick, I had turned the place into a murder scene.

# C.R.E.A.M. 3

# CHAPTER 12
## NIC

I PASSED THE DROP OFF SPOT just to peep the scene out before turning in. Tray's bitch ass really had a nigga fucked up sending a nigga alone. I guessed it was a test to see what happened. I was definitely gonna need the nigga to know I wasn't gonna be used as no muthafuckin' bait though 'cause that's exactly what it seemed like was happening. I didn't know what had gotten into that fool questioning my loyalty and my work. Shit, I was the same nigga from day one.

I went against what Tray considered to be "his better judgment" and picked up my lil cousin, Darrius, to ride with me. Darrius was a known stick-up kid around Baton Rouge. Tray didn't trust or care too much about him, and he would never approve of him. But fuck it, the nigga was blood and I knew for facts nigga had my back. So fuck what the fuck that nigga Tray was talking about.

"Cuz, what's the deal with this shit?" Darrius asked with a Choppa sitting openly on his lap.

"Mane, me and Tray hit a big lick so I'm here to pick up that bag," I said, as I pulled into the abandoned house. I realized we'd made good timing because Cache was nowhere in sight.

"A big lick? Bitch nigga, what kinda lick and how much money we talking?" Darrius asked.

"Damn, pussy, you asking too many questions. Just do what the fuck I asked you to do and chill, nigga. I already told you what I was gonna pay you." I smacked my lips at his impatient ass.

"Aight, nigga, I'ma chill for now, but you better be greasing my hands handsomely or I'ma forget you my muthafuckin' cousin, ya heard me?" I ignored what he *thought* was a threat. My mind was on one thing and one thing only—getting that money.

See, I came from a long line of pimps, hoes, and hustlers. We didn't give a fuck how we had to get that bag as long as we obtained it at the end of the day. So as I said that bullshit Darious was coming out the side of his neck with was pointless. I had plans on delivering my end of the bargain. The fool just better have my back at the end of this day.

My mind drifted back to when all the shit first happened and how I had been brought smack dab in the middle of a street beef I had nothing to do with. CO was dead and gone thanks to Cache, and by association, I accumulated a two-million-dollar debt that had nothing to do with me. I didn't fuck with the nigga CO and I didn't know him that well. However, Tray was my nigga and we were thick as thieves, and I would have fucked up the world for my nigga. But lately it was like the nigga had been throwing too much shade and it was too cloudy for that shit.

With that being said, I had to do what I had to do and decided to go with my move on Tray, straight up.

The day I slithered by Mark's crib was the day I knew that my friendship and my brother hood was over with Tray. I kept bickering, arguing, and complaining just so the nigga would give me a reason for going with the move I'd set in motion.

I was tired of the nigga threating me like I was Hebrew. Someone had to show his bitch ass that slavery was definitely over and I didn't mind being the one. I'd made a deal with the devil. I lied of course when I told Mark Tray didn't have any plans whatsoever to come up off that loot and he felt that the debt wasn't his to settle. So in return, Mark employed me as a hit for hire and placed a big fat ass bag on the nigga's dome that I gladly accepted.

"Yo, cuz, is that the nigga we waiting on pulling up right now?" Darrius asked as he pulled me out of my thoughts.

"Yeah, my nigga, that's the bitch, let's ride Clyde," I said pulling the mask over my head. Darrius followed suit. I made sure to protect my identity at all times when I dealt with that broad.

Once she was parked, she hopped out with a gun in hand. *Damn, that bitch is sexier in person.* I had spied on her Instagram page and I had to admit the gram did her no justice, especially seeing her in person.

"Bitch, you jumping out the car with that heat but where the fuck is the bag? Huh?" Darrius crazy ass asked before I could say anything, as if *he* was the head nigga in charge.

"Chill, nigga," I said, letting the nigga know to stand down and that I was the captain of the ship.

"Where is my daughter?" Cache asked, cutting straight to the chase. Out of the corner of my eye, I watched Darrius to see his reaction. *The nigga didn't even flinch*, I thought, *coldhearted muthafucka.*

"She good, ma. But you and I both know we didn't come here for no questions. You know you won't get your daughter until we get this money," I said standing my ground.

"Where is Tray?" she asked, as I watched her bottom lip tremble. I couldn't distinguish whether it was pain, fear, or hurt. Before I answered her question, I thought about what I wanted to say, no, what I *needed* to say before I said it. I had already made up my mind that Tray ass was good and ex-ed out. I wasn't in the business for picking up beef, especially another nigga's at that. I didn't give a fuck, friend or foe. There was only two things in the world that I actually gave two fucks about and that was getting money and pussy.

"The nigga couldn't be here but there has also been a change of plans," I told her, as I watched her facial expression convert to worry.

"What do you mean? Please, don't hurt my baby!" She pleaded with me and I watched the gun tremble in her hand as if she was losing her nerve.

"Nah, lil momma, it ain't that type of party. I just want that bag and I hope yo ass ain't playing no games 'cause I ain't here for the fuckery.

"Look, I got your money in the trunk. Every bit of the one million dollars I said I would brin—

"Hold up, muthafucka! One million dollars? As in two commas and six zeros?" Darrius asked, cutting Cache off mid-sentence. She shook her head *yes* before I could stop her from responding to the nigga's question. "Oh yeah, cuz, you wasn't never lying when you said a big lick. Bitch, who you are again? Damn, cuzzo, I wasn't expecting a big payday like this!" Darrius said, excitedly rubbing his hands together as if he was sitting at the table about to demolish a meal fit for a king. I knew the nigga wasn't expecting us to be coming to snatch up a mill so there had definitely been a change of plans.

*Pst! Pst! Pst!*

I wasted no time lifting my 9mm with the silencer on it.

"Uuuggh, fuck! Nigga you shot me!" Darrius hit the ground not knowing whether to hold his chest or stomach. I looked and saw the blood as it began to cover his shirt the color of crimson. "What the fuck you do that for, nigga?" he asked, trying to use the little strength he had left to pull the trigger of his Chopper. But the nigga never had the chance to do so …

*Pow! Pow!* I hadn't gotten the chance to pull my trigger. I looked over at Cache and knew it had been her who'd done the honors. I didn't know whether to shoot the bitch or shake the bitch's hand.

"I just want my daughter back and I could clearly see how this was about to turn out if I hadn't done it. Out of the two of you, I could tell you were the HNIC. He was lost at what was really going down and I couldn't take a chance on him pulling the trigger before you," she said waiting on my response.

"Bitch, that was my cousin!" Were the first words that left my lips. For the first time since I'd shot Darrius, I noticed Cache had a bag thrown over her shoulders. She pulled it off and tossed it between us.

"And A'miracle is my child," she said without blinking or flinching," The rest of your money is in the trunk. I'ma get it so we can move on. And cousin or no cousin, we all playing a game with the chance of losing or winning. And besides, if I hadn't pulled the trigger you was definitely going to do it. You should be thanking me though because at least you don't have to face your family and live the rest of your life with his blood on your hands. Now I can clearly see that it's every man for himself. We can either do this two ways or one. You can take this money for yourself plus the other four million, and keep it all for yourself in exchange of me getting my baby back unharmed, and you can bring me the head of that snake ass bitch Tray." I thought about it for a second. Honestly, it was already on my mind to give her that crying ass baby back, kill Tray, and run off with the million bucks. But shit, five would definitely do the body good like a tall glass of milk. It didn't take me long whatsoever to think about the shit.

"Aight," I said, extending my hand to shake on it as if we had just made a genuine business deal. And in a way we had, because I was never down with kidnapping no muthafuckin' baby from jump.

"OK, but for the other four mill you gotta put a lil work in for," she said, shaking my hand. I didn't give a fuck what kinda work a nigga had to put in. I would soon be five million dollars richer, and right about now if we had to roll up on Erica Faye she could get it too. *Nah*, I thought, shaking my head. I couldn't kill my own momma but then again …

After accepting and agreeing with getting that money with Cache, I hopped back in the car and left Darrius laid out on the ground wondering if I had done the right thing. But something in my gut told me I had just made a deal with the devil.

Cache

I WAS FEELING VERY OPTIMISTIC after last night's exchange. I'd left knowing that shit had certainly converted for the better. Dealing with them niggas in the streets had become one of my better professions and I couldn't help but see right through that clown. I could literally see the dollar signs in his eyes and knew he was after more than just receiving a cut out of the money that he and Tray acquired from me. The nigga wanted the whole pie, and just like our Heavenly Father promised everlasting life, I had served him the crème de la crème every hustler searched for in life. The best, the finest, and he had accepted becoming a serpent for the love of money.

I was sure the lick we were about to hit would go well. Chanel had set the scenery for the perfect heist while her and Mark took a trip to Kingston, the capital of Jamaica. I was ready to get the shit over with so I could really retire from the streets. After this was all said and done and I tied all loose ends, I was leaving the states and meeting Chanel in Jamaica. No way was I going to remain a sitting duck for the next nigga to come and destroy what was left of me. The bullshit that Tray pulled had shown me the streets remembered my walk

# C.R.E.A.M. 3

and I should walk lightly, especially knowing I wanted to pull out of the game and no longer wanted any parts of it.

## Chanel

JAMAICA WAS PEACEFUL. That was my first thought as soon as I stepped on the Caribbean soil. The life I lived with Mark was the life little girls dreamed of, and there I was living my best life. It really fucked my head up that I was going against my better judgement falling right into the shoes of my sister. We were supposed to be breaking the cycle but there I was egging the shit on.

"Hey baby, what you thinking about? You look like you have a lot on your mind. Don't tell me you back to having second thoughts," Mark asked me, when he stepped behind me to wrap me in his arms.

"No, baby, not at all. I'm having thoughts but it's not what you are thinking," I said, as I started to melt in his firm embrace.

"Well penny for your thoughts?" he said in my ear then kissed my neck as we detached from one another.

"Oh, baby, it's just that you treat me so nice and no one has ever been this authentic. You cater to my every need without me even having to ask. So baby, if I made you feel like I wasn't as happy as you are to be a parent to the child," I said touching my stomach, "no correction, *our* child, then I'm sorry. I truly apologize for not showing as much passion as you showed. I was just surprised. But I just want you to know that I love you and I love the baby we created," I said. And as soon as I'd spoke the last words, tears fell from my eyes.

"Damn, baby," Mark said, as he came out of his right pocket with a black velvet box and positioned himself on bended knee," I'm so glad you spoke those words because, no lie, for a minute, you had a nigga feeling like you had some regrets. But now that you've said what you said, I know I'm making the right decision so ... would you marry me?"

*Oh fuck, lawd why me!* I thought. "I gotta call Cache!" I ran off. I had to put a stop to this!

# CHAPTER 13
## CACHE

"Alright, nigga, first things first. I need my daughter back in my arms before any more money is exchanged from my hand to yours."

"What the fuck you mean?" he asked cutting game off. "That wasn't the fuckin' deal," Nic said, letting me know he wasn't feeling what I had said.

"Well nigga, deals change all the time, so what? Plus, you done x-ed yo nigga out and it's a good thing too because you definitely on the winning team. And whether you get with the program or not, I'm still getting my daughter back," I said, trying to contain my anger, because on some shit, I still had to play by some of the nigga's rules. I couldn't become completely sporty, just like his bitch ass turned on his boy, he could turn on me with a snap of a finger.

"How I know you ain't gone play no fuckin' game?" he asked me seriously.

"I'ma be real with you. There's no honor amongst thieves, and as far as me playing games? Nigga you got a million muthafuckin' dollars! Muthafuckas kill for way less. Just tell me where my daughter is so we can move forward and get this shit over with," I said, staring the nigga down. He was silent for what seemed like an eternity.

"A'ight, you know what? I'ma follow your lead 'cause I'm sick of yo crying ass brat anyway. And honestly, I wasn't down with this shit from jump, so fuck it, let's do this shit. We can ride in yo whip," he said, agreeing with me. But there was one thing …

"Man, we ride in your car."

"How you gonna get back?" Nic asked me.

"Damn, nigga, all that shit should be the least of your worries, let's go," I said, stepping over his people making sure not not step in dry blood. Then I walked to the passenger's side of the car.

***

WITHIN THAN FIVE MINUTES we had pulled up to a house. "Is this where my daughter been the whole time?" I asked. My mind wondered if she had been treated right, had she eaten, or if she'd been hurt in any way.

"Yeah, this is where she's been." He answered just as my phone had begun to vibrate in my hand. I looked down at the screen and saw that Chanel was the caller. I pressed the ignore button because I was in the middle of something very important. I knew she was just checking on me to see if I had hit Mark's house but I didn't have time to be speaking all reckless over the phone about the shit.

"You ready?" Nic asked as I placed my phone in my back pocket.

"Born," I responded. I cocked my gun and placed a bullet in the chamber. I said a quick prayer before stepping out of the car. I knew that moment was do-or-die.

### Nic

I LOOKED AROUND THE DARK STREETS before we both stepped out of the car. I was ready to get the shit over with and move on with my life. I couldn't help but thank God that this hoe Cache hadn't tried nothing slick because the shit would have turned out horrible. Smart girl!

I walked in the house and headed to the front bedroom. I saw Tray laying down as peacefully as ever, without a care in the world. If only he knew today would his last day on earth and there was nothing he could do about it because I had already made a deal with the devil. Beside him, the baby lay only a few inches away and she was asleep also and had the same expression on her face. I had to hurry up and get the shit out of the way before I lost my nerves to go through with it. I crept up to the bed and raised my gun.

"Nigga, what the fuck you doing?" was the only thing Tray got out of his mouth before I pulled the trigger putting him back to sleep forever.

Cache

*NIGGA, WHAT THE FUCK YOU DOING?* I'd heard Tray ask Nic. "What the fuck that nigga doing?" I mumbled and questioned myself. *Was he folding? Was both of them muthafuckas about to get at me?* Just as the thoughts raced through my mind like NASCAR, I heard my baby's cry followed by a gunshot. Without a second thought, I kicked the door in using all the strength I had left within me. I quickly did an inventory of the room. My main concern was A'miracle. With the exception of her, I pumped bullets in whatever and whoever moved.

"Aaahh, fuck, I'm shot!" I yelled, realizing I'd allowed Nic to get a shot off. I had completed the mission I had come for as I watched Nic and Tray bleed out. I held the side of my stomach as I cried tears of joy.

"Ma-ma." A'miracle cried as she reached for me. She had only been gone for a few weeks but the shit felt like a lifetime. As I held the side of my stomach to prevent so much blood from flowing, I limped over to the side of the bed my daughter was on. I picked her up and held her on the opposite side of my injury.

Before walking out of the bedroom, I looked back one more time and knew it was some shit I never wanted to go through again.

## Yolanda Moore

"Freeze! Put your fuckin' hands up now!" I heard as soon as I stepped out into the crisp night air. I dropped the gun on the ground because I definitely wasn't trying to go out in a blaze of glory. Fuck what ya heard. That shit only happens in movies like *Set it Off* or *Takers*.

A female and male officer ran up with guns pointed. Their comrades waited, ducked off behind some police cruisers with flashing lights, until I was apprehended. The female grabbed A'miracle out of my arms, and as soon as my arms were snatched behind my back to be handcuffed everything went black.

\*\*\*

WHEN I CAME TO, I WAS LAID UP in the hospital with one hand cuffed to the bed. I wasn't surprised that this had been my destiny. I was probably charged with the murders of Latray and Nico. Even though I wasn't the one who had actually pulled the trigger on Tray, them bitches (police) wasn't going to want to hear my story about my kid being kidnapped. I mean, after all, I definitely wasn't considered an upstanding influencer of the Baton Rouge community.

"Cache Price," I heard someone call as the door was being opened. Wasn't no reason for me to respond. Fuck, I mean, they knew I was there. I kept my face toward the window not even bothering to look up and see who had walked in.

"My name is Detective Fernandez. I'm with Baton Rouge homicide," I heard the detective say but still refused to say anything. "Well you don't have to say anything. I'll do the talking. So about six months ago when you and Antonio Clark ran to Mexico, we started looking into your case, trying to build it actually.

But I must admit you're a smart girl. Just when we would have enough evidence to lock you up and throw away the key, somehow we would be thrown off your trail and end up having to arrest someone else for the crime instead. But when the chase started all over again, so then you had called your friend Klimax to go into an offshore account with a couple of million tucked away for a rainy day." When he said Klimax's name the shit surely grabbed my attention, so I turned my head and found myself looking into a familiar face. It was the same man I'd seen Klimax with that day he got out of that black Charger.

"Klimax was working undercover, he's a cop," Detective Fernandez said, causing my pressure to shoot up. I couldn't believe that muthafucka had played us like that. I wonder if Chanel knew that shit? Nah, fuck no, she would never do such a thing. "He was only doing his job, Cache. That's what we do, our job. But good thing we were ..." The nigga was crazy if he thought I should've been grateful that they were doing their job. "We know you didn't kill Latray but you are responsible for killing Nico. But we also know for good reason. Klimax had gathered enough information for you to walk free of charge. We knew they had taken your daughter and you had done what every mother should," he said, as he got up and uncuffed my hand from the bed.

"Are you serious?" I asked, sitting up in the bed now.

"Yes, bitch!" Klimax said, walking through the door as soon as the words left my mouth. He walked over and handed me a phone. I was hesitant at first because I definitely didn't trust his ass any more, but then I thought about how he'd helped me the whole time. I grabbed the phone.

"Hello?"

"Sis, he asked me to marry him and I said yes!" Chanel screamed through the phone. I couldn't say anything. I was at a loss for words because I knew we were the last of a dying breed and we both could live happily. I was glad I didn't have to rob Mark in order to get the money for A'miracle because my sister wouldn't have been telling me her good news.

"Where are my babies, sis?" I asked as my voice cracked, hoping for the best.

"Right here with my, sis, so don't worry. Get well soon, so you can get back to us ... love you." I could hear her smiling through her words.

"Love you too." I gave Klimax his phone back.

"I have one more thing for you," he said, giving me the duffle bags I'd given to Nic the night everything happened. I cut my eyes up at the other detective not knowing if it was safe to accept the bag.

"You good," he said smiling. They walked out of the room, leaving me to think about how grateful I was to still have my freedom.

## CHAPTER 14
### CACHE

*1 year later…*

I dabbed the sweat beading above my top lip with the back of my hand. I really wished I was doing something else right now. Instead, I was at my desk contemplating if I should write this for my children. The more I thought about leaving my children to have to fend for themselves in this cold world, the more my stomach sank. I picked up my pink pen, the pink sparkly one A'Miracle loved to play with and willed myself to write the words embedded on my heart. I was really struggling to get them down on paper. I felt as though writing down my thoughts would be saying fuck life rather than continuing to be the soulja Ann created.

*I'm a fighter. So, what am I doing here?* It was as if I was ready to give in. My kids deserved more right now. This, what I was doing, wasn't a consideration of suicide. I wouldn't dare commit the ultimate sin against myself and God, but if I couldn't get up and fight, then I might as well have been the fuckin' flop everyone was claiming me to be.

"Quit being a pussy," I said aloud, trying to gain control of the emotion as it oozed out of my pores like an infectious disease.

"Just write the book, Cache. Only two things can happen in the trenches … kill or be killed," I said, having a full-fledged conversation with myself. I began to write despite what my heart told me. If I had to leave this world I wanted my children to have the realest, most honest truth. The one thing I had found out was that money didn't always bring you happiness. Maybe in the moment, but once it was all said and done, money couldn't buy me love or happiness. The streets had taken away what I loved.

# Yolanda Moore

*Identity* was the first word I wrote down to begin my story. My memoir. Just in case. So, I started to jot my thoughts down. It began: *Dead, gone rapt, absent, astray. Damned, doomed, vanished, desperate and destroyed. Everything I feel: VOID. I always knew this would be life for me, especially with all I had taken in as a child. Still, I fought for the better ... my better. I fought so hard with unannounced strength, but still, I headed into destruction. With no guidance (someone who leads or directs another) to tell me the fight I fought was against myself. I was faced with another me, someone I would like to label a beast, but didn't know how to defeat myself.*

*Because the scripture: "the truth shall set you free," was something I had been taught early in life, it was embedded in me, yet I was too ashamed to admit the things I had done in the dark. I robbed, I stole, and I committed adultery. I was so ashamed of myself ... lack of self-confidence with no confidence.*

*At the age of fourteen is when it all started, and I had taken a left turn long before I was granted the chance of adolescence. I'd had my first experience with consuming drugs, but it seemed I was destined for havoc long before that. You would've thought I knew better. I watched my mom and dad, your grandparents, go through some horrific things in life, suffering through addiction. Seeing them do drugs and drink alcohol, which caused them to lose their lives at a young age, apparently wasn't enough for me.*

*My drug addiction, in a way, had caused me to lose a lot too. Hope, preservation, truth, and so on. I'm grateful that I'm able to see and overcome what my parents could not—and that is to defeat the stronghold of addiction. What helped me faithfully through my recovery when I was in prison was the Eight Beatitudes (R.E.C.O.V.E.R.Y).*

# C.R.E.A.M. 3

*Here is my story on how I gained the whole world just to lose it.*

1) *Realize I'm not God. I admit that I am powerless to control my tendency to do the wrong things and that my life is unmanageable. "Happy are those who know they are spiritually poor" (Matt 5:3).*

Life started moving for me in a promiscuous way, too recklessly. Looking for what I lacked ... LOVE. Men and drugs became my antidote and even women too, but above all Xanax and coke were my GODs, cleansing and washing away the sins that sustained my skin. My drug abuse is where I found refuge. With it, it was as if a blanket covered my mind and heart. I felt safe. At least that was what I thought at the moment.

It was a feeling I had never sensed, and I had finally fell in love with myself. I felt as if there was an aura about me that boosted my confidence. I was able to do things I never imagined—like look in the mirror and love what I saw. I was five feet seven and walked with a stride Naomi Campbell couldn't even touch. I started wearing makeup, and little by little, exposing my body. It made me feel superior. No one could tell me anything. I was that bitch.

2) *Earnestly believe that God exists, that I matter to him and that he has the power to help me recover. "Happy are those who mourn for they shall be comforted" (Matt 5:4).*

Yeah, that was until the truth was exposed. By the time I longed to get my life together I had become a mother of two and shit started to get too demanding. You would have thought this would be a time when I ran to the altar and hooked up with the Holy Spirit, but now I was faced with the same blessings and curse that fell upon my mother. I had two beautiful children, but my life had started to crumble like a cookie. I wasn't worried about much though because like I said, drugs had become my ally, my accountability partner.

    3)    Consciously choose to commit all my life and will to Christ's care and control. "Happy are the meek" (Matt 5:5).

I started to feel as though I wasn't worthy of much in life because I had done the unforgivable to myself. In a flash, my mother's life had become my destiny. I remember trying not to fall into the pits of hell, but somehow I ended up falling directly into her footsteps while taking it all in stride. My life had become a constant simulation and I was trapped inside a landscape of fear, which had converted into my reality. Just like Tris, in the Divergent series, I had become accustomed to life, but knew I didn't belong, but I still fought.
    I didn't give up. "God makes no mistakes," is what I told myself constantly, and I knew He had given me the strength to fight with the heart of a lion— all I had to do was hear my roar. At that moment I didn't know what I possessed. With all that said, the thought of it all made me decree the assassination against my demonic entity. All that existed in my past cast an attack on my future before I knew what hit me. I knew I needed to get through and remain standing once the smoke had cleared.

    4)    Openly examine and confess my faults to myself, to God, and someone I trust. "Happy are the pure in heart" (Matt 5:8).

## C.R.E.A.M. 3

*A future I thought I wouldn't be able to make it through, I was faced with armed robbery, and a murder case over my head I did not commit. I spent several years of my life facing a life sentence. Honestly, I thought I would never fear anything, but I was afraid, which was a feeling I hadn't felt in years. Of course, without self-medicating, I also felt exposed. I became overwhelmed with emotion like when God opened the floodgates of Heaven. I was filled with dread. However, my criminal activity was not on my cranium. All the hurt, the pain, and the abuse I faced was now my challenge. Crying for days had been similar to how a duck takes to water. I remember calling home and telling Momo C.W. how ashamed I was. Without Xanax I was now really able to look in the mirror and see the truth, and not the mirror that showed my physical appearance.*

*When fighting for my life in the 19th Judicial System was all said and done, I had been sentenced to a fifteen-year sentence of hard labor. I knew I had a lot of work to do. I was determined to walk a different walk to talk a different talk, and this time I didn't need drugs to boost my self-esteem. I had been blessed with charm and I knew exactly how to beat the system.*

5)    *Voluntarily submit to every change God wants to make in my life and humbly ask Him to remove my character defects. "Happy are those whose greatest desire is to do what God requires" (Matt 5:6).*

One thing my mother had always taught me was how to survive. So, I considered myself a survivor, an overcomer, and I knew how to endure and outlast everything thrown in my path. I knew to survive I had to always keep on keeping on. See, finding a way to get through the storm was something I never had a problem with. One of my favorite sayings was about dancing and rejoicing in the rain. I had flirted with death for far too long. I wanted to see life— my life through a kaleidoscope, up close and personal. The only way I could do so was if I took time out with myself. So I stopped placing all my hurts and hang-ups on the front line, while carrying everyone else's baggage around, and I looked into the two mirrors of my life's kaleidoscope and examined all my faults. I knew what I had to do. Those loose bits of colored glass had been shattered for far too long. Besides, I knew I couldn't help others if I couldn't help myself.

6) Evaluate all my relationships. Offer forgiveness to those who have hurt me and make amends for harm I've done to others, except when to do so would harm them or others. "Happy are the merciful" (Matt 5:7). "Happy are the peacemakers" (Matt 5:9).

I had started to forgive everyone who had caused me harm, whether it had been mentally, physically, sexually, or even spiritually. Well let's just say the people who were supposed to have been my protectors hadn't played their parts. Including myself because I realized I had done myself the most harm. Naturally, once I forgave myself I started to heal as if I had touched the hem of God's garment. The relationship between my family and I did a three-sixty, which included my mother with whom my hurt had generated, and her mother as well. However, I cannot just stop there. Asking for forgiveness from the two of you is the hardest, but I know it has to be done. I'm not sure what the future holds for me but I feel this is just as appropriate time as any other. Forgive me of my transgressions? At least, I hope the two of you will find it in your hearts.

# C.R.E.A.M. 3

*As I said, this is a generational curse and our family wears it proudly without even knowing it. Maybe one day you can have a life with kids, a yard with a dog, and a white-picket fence. Or maybe that only happens on TV shows like "Full House" with Joey, or "The Brady Bunch." What I'm trying to get at is I want the best for my babies as long as it comes in the form of peace, joy, happiness, and most importantly, loyalty. Not love, because love, loves no one but self. Always remember that. And if one of you so happen to prove me wrong, then so be it.*

*7)     Reserve a daily time with God for self-examination. Bible reading and prayer in order to know God and His will for my life and to gain the power to follow His will.*

*Yes, my first step was admitting I was powerless, but my first step was also cracking open my celebrate recovery workbook and continuing to turn the pages. Well, that was until I had been granted early release. I never made it through the whole 8 steps so if I had to figure things out on my own I would, but the saying 'God forgives not me' ...*

Coming out of my thoughts, I stopped writing the memoir and decided my work here was done. The more I wrote the more I felt as if I was writing my end, as if I was planning my own demise.
"Get it together, Cache," I told myself.
As I stood up, I felt a cold chill throughout my body as if death was creeping around the corner. I made up my mind to go and peek in the room to make sure my kids were sound asleep, and that no harm had come their way. Just when the thought crossed my mind, I heard the wooden floors creak and remembered Tony had made a quick run to the store.

# Yolanda Moore

"Fuck." I cursed under my breath so low I barely heard myself. *My gun,* I thought, as I tried to tiptoe through the house. I had left it in the kitchen on top of the island. *So fuckin' reckless of me,* I thought, angry at myself for slipping up like this. But this was the type of shit that happened when you were in your heart wearing your feelings on your sleeve. Everything that was supposed to matter faded. I had been trying so hard to keep my head on straight and stay alive for my children, I had become too engrossed with the fatality of fuckin' up. I just hoped the slip of the mind wouldn't cost me my life.

Just as I crossed the threshold to enter the living room, I saw Knasir standing by the TV with the remote in his hand. Out the corner of my eye I saw a shadow and my heart dropped into my ass.

*Boom! Boom! Boom!* I heard the gunshots.

I ran into the direction of the front door. I swung it open and that's when I saw Tony and Maya dead on the ground. Karma had finally caught up with both of them. I couldn't do anything but laugh to keep from crying because I knew my time would come soon. How soon? I didn't know but out of all of the life lessons, I had been taught that damage is irreparable and it's a cold little world we live in—a world filled with self-serving individuals. If you wanna stay on top, you gotta watch your own back even if it means getting your enemies to eliminate each other.

The thought made me think of The 48 Laws of Power, a book by Robert Greene. Law 7 advises us: *"Get others to do the work for you, but always take the credit.* Use the wisdom, knowledge, and leg work of other people to further your own cause. Not only will such assistance save you valuable time and energy, it will give you a God-like aura of efficiency and speed. In the end your helpers will be forgotten and you will be remembered. Never do yourself what others can do for you."

Like I said, I wasn't God and I still haven't found the courage to forgive. I thought as I went to grab the phone to call 911. I'm no longer a product of the streets. I am now a mother, an author, and I am ready to tell my story and I will leave a legacy for my children about how "Cash. Ruled. Everything. Around. Me."

The End.

Yolanda Moore

**Lock Down Publications and Ca$h Presents** assisted publishing packages.

### BASIC PACKAGE $499
Editing
Cover Design
Formatting

### UPGRADED PACKAGE $800
Typing
Editing
Cover Design
Formatting

### ADVANCE PACKAGE $1,200
Typing
Editing
Cover Design
Formatting
Copyright registration
Proofreading
Upload book to Amazon

### LDP SUPREME PACKAGE $1,500
Typing
Editing
Cover Design

C.R.E.A.M. 3

Formatting
Copyright registration
Proofreading
Set up Amazon account
Upload book to Amazon
Advertise on LDP Amazon and Facebook page

***Other services available upon request. Additional charges may apply
**Lock Down Publications**
**P.O. Box 944**
**Stockbridge, GA 30281-9998**
**Phone # 470 303-9761**

Yolanda Moore

## Submission Guideline

Submit the first three chapters of your completed manuscript to ldpsubmissions@gmail.com, subject line: Your book's title. The manuscript must be in a .doc file and sent as an attachment. Document should be in Times New Roman, double spaced and in size 12 font. Also, provide your synopsis and full contact information. If sending multiple submissions, they must each be in a separate email.

Have a story but no way to send it electronically? You can still submit to LDP/Ca$h Presents. Send in the first three chapters, written or typed, of your completed manuscript to:

**LDP: Submissions Dept**
**Po Box 944**
**Stockbridge, Ga 30281**

*DO NOT send original manuscript. Must be a duplicate.*

Provide your synopsis and a cover letter containing your full contact information.

Thanks for considering LDP and Ca$h Presents.

# C.R.E.A.M. 3

## **NEW RELEASES**

BORN IN THE GRAVE by SELF MADE TAY
MOAN IN MY MOUTH by XTASY
SKI MASK MONEY by RENTA
C.R.E.A.M. 3 by YOLANDA MOORE

Yolanda Moore

**Coming Soon from Lock Down Publications/Ca$h Presents**
BLOOD OF A BOSS VI
SHADOWS OF THE GAME II
TRAP BASTARD II
By **Askari**
LOYAL TO THE GAME **IV**
By **T.J. & Jelissa**
TRUE SAVAGE **VIII**
MIDNIGHT CARTEL IV
DOPE BOY MAGIC IV
CITY OF KINGZ III
NIGHTMARE ON SILENT AVE II
THE PLUG OF LIL MEXICO II
CLASSIC CITY II
By **Chris Green**
BLAST FOR ME **III**
A SAVAGE DOPEBOY III
CUTTHROAT MAFIA III
DUFFLE BAG CARTEL VII
HEARTLESS GOON VI
By **Ghost**
A HUSTLER'S DECEIT III
KILL ZONE II
BAE BELONGS TO ME III
TIL DEATH II
By **Aryanna**
KING OF THE TRAP III

# C.R.E.A.M. 3

By **T.J. Edwards**
GORILLAZ IN THE BAY V
3X KRAZY III
STRAIGHT BEAST MODE III
**De'Kari**
KINGPIN KILLAZ IV
STREET KINGS III
PAID IN BLOOD III
CARTEL KILLAZ IV
DOPE GODS III
**Hood Rich**
SINS OF A HUSTLA II
**ASAD**
RICH $AVAGE II
**By Martell Troublesome Bolden**
YAYO V
Bred In The Game 2
**S. Allen**
THE STREETS WILL TALK II
**By Yolanda Moore**
SON OF A DOPE FIEND III
HEAVEN GOT A GHETTO II
SKI MASK MONEY II
**By Renta**
LOYALTY AIN'T PROMISED III
**By Keith Williams**
I'M NOTHING WITHOUT HIS LOVE II

Yolanda Moore

SINS OF A THUG II
TO THE THUG I LOVED BEFORE II
IN A HUSTLER I TRUST II

**By Monet Dragun**

QUIET MONEY IV
EXTENDED CLIP III
THUG LIFE IV

By **Trai'Quan**

THE STREETS MADE ME IV

By **Larry D. Wright**

IF YOU CROSS ME ONCE II
ANGEL IV

By **Anthony Fields**

THE STREETS WILL NEVER CLOSE IV

**By K'ajji**

HARD AND RUTHLESS III
KILLA KOUNTY III

**By Khufu**

MONEY GAME III

**By Smoove Dolla**

JACK BOYS VS DOPE BOYS II
A GANGSTA'S QUR'AN V
COKE GIRLZ II
COKE BOYS II

**By Romell Tukes**

MURDA WAS THE CASE II

**Elijah R. Freeman**

# C.R.E.A.M. 3

THE STREETS NEVER LET GO II
**By Robert Baptiste**
AN UNFORESEEN LOVE IV
By **Meesha**
KING OF THE TRENCHES III
by **GHOST & TRANAY ADAMS**

MONEY MAFIA II
By **Jibril Williams**
QUEEN OF THE ZOO III
By **Black Migo**
VICIOUS LOYALTY III
**By Kingpen**
A GANGSTA'S PAIN III
**By J-Blunt**
CONFESSIONS OF A JACKBOY III
**By Nicholas Lock**
GRIMEY WAYS III
**By Ray Vinci**
KING KILLA II
**By Vincent "Vitto" Holloway**
BETRAYAL OF A THUG II
**By Fre$h**
THE MURDER QUEENS II
**By Michael Gallon**
THE BIRTH OF A GANGSTER III
**By Delmont Player**
TREAL LOVE II

Yolanda Moore

**By Le'Monica Jackson**
FOR THE LOVE OF BLOOD II
**By Jamel Mitchell**
RAN OFF ON DA PLUG II
**By Paper Boi Rari**
HOOD CONSIGLIERE II
**By Keese**
PRETTY GIRLS DO NASTY THINGS II
**By Nicole Goosby**
PROTÉGÉ OF A LEGEND II
**By Corey Robinson**
IT'S JUST ME AND YOU II
**By Ah'Million**
**BORN IN THE GRAVE II**
**By Self Made Tay**

## Available Now

RESTRAINING ORDER **I & II**
By **CA$H & Coffee**
LOVE KNOWS NO BOUNDARIES **I II & III**
By **Coffee**
RAISED AS A GOON I, II, III & IV
BRED BY THE SLUMS I, II, III

# C.R.E.A.M. 3

BLAST FOR ME I & II
ROTTEN TO THE CORE I II III
A BRONX TALE I, II, III
DUFFLE BAG CARTEL I II III IV V VI
HEARTLESS GOON I II III IV V
A SAVAGE DOPEBOY I II
DRUG LORDS I II III
CUTTHROAT MAFIA I II
KING OF THE TRENCHES
By **Ghost**
LAY IT DOWN **I & II**
LAST OF A DYING BREED I II
BLOOD STAINS OF A SHOTTA I & II III
By **Jamaica**
LOYAL TO THE GAME I II III
LIFE OF SIN I, II III
By **TJ & Jelissa**
BLOODY COMMAS I & II
SKI MASK CARTEL I  II & III
KING OF NEW YORK I II,III IV V
RISE TO POWER I II III
COKE KINGS I II III IV V
BORN HEARTLESS I II III IV
KING OF THE TRAP I II
By **T.J. Edwards**
IF LOVING HIM IS WRONG…I & II
LOVE ME EVEN WHEN IT HURTS I II III

# Yolanda Moore

### By **Jelissa**
WHEN THE STREETS CLAP BACK I & II III
THE HEART OF A SAVAGE I II III IV
MONEY MAFIA
LOYAL TO THE SOIL I II III

### By **Jibril Williams**
A DISTINGUISHED THUG STOLE MY HEART I II & III
LOVE SHOULDN'T HURT I II III IV
RENEGADE BOYS I II III IV
PAID IN KARMA I II III
SAVAGE STORMS I II III
AN UNFORESEEN LOVE I II III

### By **Meesha**
A GANGSTER'S CODE I &, II III
A GANGSTER'S SYN I II III
THE SAVAGE LIFE I II III
CHAINED TO THE STREETS I II III
BLOOD ON THE MONEY I II III
A GANGSTA'S PAIN I II

### By **J-Blunt**
PUSH IT TO THE LIMIT

### By **Bre' Hayes**
BLOOD OF A BOSS **I, II, III, IV, V**
SHADOWS OF THE GAME
TRAP BASTARD

### By **Askari**
THE STREETS BLEED MURDER **I, II & III**

# C.R.E.A.M. 3

THE HEART OF A GANGSTA I II& III
By **Jerry Jackson**
CUM FOR ME I II III IV V VI VII VIII
An **LDP Erotica Collaboration**
BRIDE OF A HUSTLA **I II & II**
THE FETTI GIRLS **I, II& III**
CORRUPTED BY A GANGSTA I, II III, IV
BLINDED BY HIS LOVE
THE PRICE YOU PAY FOR LOVE I, II ,III
DOPE GIRL MAGIC I II III
By **Destiny Skai**
WHEN A GOOD GIRL GOES BAD
By **Adrienne**
THE COST OF LOYALTY I II III
**By Kweli**
A GANGSTER'S REVENGE **I II III & IV**
THE BOSS MAN'S DAUGHTERS I II III IV V
A SAVAGE LOVE **I & II**
BAE BELONGS TO ME I II
A HUSTLER'S DECEIT I, II, III
WHAT BAD BITCHES DO I, II, III
SOUL OF A MONSTER I II III
KILL ZONE
A DOPE BOY'S QUEEN I II III
TIL DEATH
By **Aryanna**
A KINGPIN'S AMBITON

# Yolanda Moore

A KINGPIN'S AMBITION II

I MURDER FOR THE DOUGH

By **Ambitious**

TRUE SAVAGE I II III IV V VI VII

DOPE BOY MAGIC I, II, III

MIDNIGHT CARTEL I II III

CITY OF KINGZ I II

NIGHTMARE ON SILENT AVE

THE PLUG OF LIL MEXICO II

CLASSIC CITY

By **Chris Green**

A DOPEBOY'S PRAYER

By **Eddie "Wolf" Lee**

THE KING CARTEL **I, II & III**

By **Frank Gresham**

THESE NIGGAS AIN'T LOYAL **I, II & III**

By **Nikki Tee**

GANGSTA SHYT **I II & III**

By **CATO**

THE ULTIMATE BETRAYAL

By **Phoenix**

BOSS'N UP **I , II & III**

By **Royal Nicole**

I LOVE YOU TO DEATH

By **Destiny J**

I RIDE FOR MY HITTA

I STILL RIDE FOR MY HITTA

# C.R.E.A.M. 3

By **Misty Holt**
LOVE & CHASIN' PAPER
By **Qay Crockett**
TO DIE IN VAIN
SINS OF A HUSTLA
By **ASAD**
BROOKLYN HUSTLAZ
By **Boogsy Morina**
BROOKLYN ON LOCK I & II
By **Sonovia**
GANGSTA CITY
By **Teddy Duke**
A DRUG KING AND HIS DIAMOND I & II III
A DOPEMAN'S RICHES
HER MAN, MINE'S TOO I, II
CASH MONEY HO'S
THE WIFEY I USED TO BE I II
PRETTY GIRLS DO NASTY THINGS
**By Nicole Goosby**
TRAPHOUSE KING **I II & III**
KINGPIN KILLAZ I II III
STREET KINGS I II
PAID IN BLOOD **I II**
CARTEL KILLAZ I II III
DOPE GODS I II
By **Hood Rich**
LIPSTICK KILLAH **I, II, III**

# Yolanda Moore

CRIME OF PASSION I II & III
FRIEND OR FOE I II III

By **Mimi**

STEADY MOBBN' **I, II, III**
THE STREETS STAINED MY SOUL I II III

By **Marcellus Allen**

WHO SHOT YA **I, II, III**
SON OF A DOPE FIEND I II
HEAVEN GOT A GHETTO
SKI MASK MONEY

**Renta**

GORILLAZ IN THE BAY **I II III IV**
TEARS OF A GANGSTA I II
3X KRAZY I II
STRAIGHT BEAST MODE I II

**DE'KARI**

TRIGGADALE I II III
MURDAROBER WAS THE CASE

**Elijah R. Freeman**

GOD BLESS THE TRAPPERS I, II, III
THESE SCANDALOUS STREETS I, II, III
FEAR MY GANGSTA I, II, III IV, V
THESE STREETS DON'T LOVE NOBODY I, II
BURY ME A G I, II, III, IV, V
A GANGSTA'S EMPIRE I, II, III, IV
THE DOPEMAN'S BODYGAURD I II
THE REALEST KILLAZ I II III

# C.R.E.A.M. 3

THE LAST OF THE OGS I II III
**Tranay Adams**
THE STREETS ARE CALLING
**Duquie Wilson**
MARRIED TO A BOSS I II III
**By Destiny Skai & Chris Green**
KINGZ OF THE GAME I II III IV V VI
**Playa Ray**
SLAUGHTER GANG I II III
RUTHLESS HEART I II III
**By Willie Slaughter**
FUK SHYT
**By Blakk Diamond**
DON'T F#CK WITH MY HEART I II
**By Linnea**
ADDICTED TO THE DRAMA I II III
IN THE ARM OF HIS BOSS II
**By Jamila**
YAYO I II III IV
A SHOOTER'S AMBITION I II
BRED IN THE GAME
**By S. Allen**
TRAP GOD I II III
RICH $AVAGE
MONEY IN THE GRAVE I II III
**By Martell Troublesome Bolden**
FOREVER GANGSTA

## Yolanda Moore

GLOCKS ON SATIN SHEETS I II
**By Adrian Dulan**
TOE TAGZ I II III IV
LEVELS TO THIS SHYT I II
IT'S JUST ME AND YOU
**By Ah'Million**
KINGPIN DREAMS I II III
RAN OFF ON DA PLUG
**By Paper Boi Rari**
CONFESSIONS OF A GANGSTA I II III IV
CONFESSIONS OF A JACKBOY I II
**By Nicholas Lock**
I'M NOTHING WITHOUT HIS LOVE
SINS OF A THUG
TO THE THUG I LOVED BEFORE
A GANGSTA SAVED XMAS
IN A HUSTLER I TRUST
**By Monet Dragun**
CAUGHT UP IN THE LIFE I II III
THE STREETS NEVER LET GO
**By Robert Baptiste**
NEW TO THE GAME I II III
MONEY, MURDER & MEMORIES I II III
By **Malik D. Rice**
LIFE OF A SAVAGE I II III
A GANGSTA'S QUR'AN I II III IV
MURDA SEASON I II III

# C.R.E.A.M. 3

GANGLAND CARTEL I II III
CHI'RAQ GANGSTAS I II III
KILLERS ON ELM STREET I II III
JACK BOYZ N DA BRONX I II III
A DOPEBOY'S DREAM I II III
JACK BOYS VS DOPE BOYS
COKE GIRLZ
COKE BOYS
**By Romell Tukes**
LOYALTY AIN'T PROMISED I II
**By Keith Williams**
QUIET MONEY I II III
THUG LIFE I II III
EXTENDED CLIP I II
By **Trai'Quan**
THE STREETS MADE ME I II III
By **Larry D. Wright**
THE ULTIMATE SACRIFICE I, II, III, IV, V, VI
KHADIFI
IF YOU CROSS ME ONCE
ANGEL I II III
IN THE BLINK OF AN EYE
By **Anthony Fields**
THE LIFE OF A HOOD STAR
**By Ca$h & Rashia Wilson**
THE STREETS WILL NEVER CLOSE I II III
**By K'ajji**

## Yolanda Moore

CREAM I II III
THE STREETS WILL TALK
**By Yolanda Moore**
NIGHTMARES OF A HUSTLA I II III
**By King Dream**
CONCRETE KILLA I II III
VICIOUS LOYALTY I II
**By Kingpen**
HARD AND RUTHLESS I II
MOB TOWN 251
THE BILLIONAIRE BENTLEYS I II III
**By Von Diesel**
GHOST MOB
**Stilloan Robinson**
MOB TIES I II III IV V VI
**By SayNoMore**
BODYMORE MURDERLAND I II III
THE BIRTH OF A GANGSTER I II
**By Delmont Player**
FOR THE LOVE OF A BOSS
**By C. D. Blue**
MOBBED UP I II III IV
THE BRICK MAN I II III IV
THE COCAINE PRINCESS I II III IV V
**By King Rio**
KILLA KOUNTY I II III
**By Khufu**

# C.R.E.A.M. 3

MONEY GAME I II
**By Smoove Dolla**
A GANGSTA'S KARMA I II
**By FLAME**
KING OF THE TRENCHES I II
by **GHOST & TRANAY ADAMS**
QUEEN OF THE ZOO I II
By **Black Migo**
GRIMEY WAYS I II
**By Ray Vinci**
XMAS WITH AN ATL SHOOTER
**By Ca$h & Destiny Skai**
KING KILLA
**By Vincent "Vitto" Holloway**
BETRAYAL OF A THUG
**By Fre$h**
THE MURDER QUEENS
**By Michael Gallon**
TREAL LOVE
**By Le'Monica Jackson**
FOR THE LOVE OF BLOOD
**By Jamel Mitchell**
HOOD CONSIGLIERE
**By Keese**
PROTÉGÉ OF A LEGEND
**By Corey Robinson**
**BORN IN THE GRAVE**

Yolanda Moore

**By Self Made Tay**
**MOAN IN MY MOUTH**
**By XTASY**

# C.R.E.A.M. 3

Yolanda Moore

## BOOKS BY LDP'S CEO, CA$H

TRUST IN NO MAN

TRUST IN NO MAN 2

TRUST IN NO MAN 3

BONDED BY BLOOD

SHORTY GOT A THUG

THUGS CRY

THUGS CRY 2

THUGS CRY 3

TRUST NO BITCH

TRUST NO BITCH 2

TRUST NO BITCH 3

TIL MY CASKET DROPS

RESTRAINING ORDER

RESTRAINING ORDER 2

IN LOVE WITH A CONVICT

LIFE OF A HOOD STAR

XMAS WITH AN ATL SHOOTER

# C.R.E.A.M. 3

CPSIA information can be obtained
at www.ICGtesting.com
Printed in the USA
LVHW011541241022
731425LV00009B/1067